SHUSAKU ENDO

Shusaku Endo was born in Japan in 1923, and spent some of his childhood in Manchuria. A convert to Catholicism early in his life, he graduated in French Literature from Keio University, and then studied for several years in Lyon.

The leading Japanese writer of today, Shusaku Endo's books include THE SEA AND POISON, WONDER-FUL FOOL, SILENCE, WHEN I WHISTLE, THE SAMURAI, STAINED GLASS ELEGIES, SCANDAL and FOREIGN STUDIES. He has been published in twenty-five countries, has won several major literary awards and received honorary doctorates from a number of American universities, and in 1981 was elected to the Nihon Geijutsuin, the Japanese Arts Academy.

sceptre

*Also by Shusaku Endo, and available
from Sceptre Books:*

FOREIGN STUDIES

Shusaku Endo

VOLCANO

Translated from the Japanese and with
an Introduction by Richard A. Schuchert

First British Commonwealth edition
published in 1978 by Peter Owen
Ltd

Sceptre edition 1992

Sceptre is an imprint of Hodder and
Stoughton Paperbacks, a division of
Hodder and Stoughton Ltd

Translated from the Japanese
Kazan

A C.I.P. catalogue for this title
is available from the British
Library

ISBN 0-340-53085-5

Printed and bound in Great Britain
for Hodder and Stoughton Paper-
backs, a division of Hodder and
Stoughton Ltd, Mill Road, Dunton
Green, Sevenoaks, Kent TN13
2YA. (Editorial Office: 47 Bedford
Square, London WC1B 3DP) by
Clays Ltd, St Ives plc. Photoset by
Rowland Phototypesetting Ltd,
Bury St Edmunds, Suffolk.

VOLCANO

INTRODUCTION

Shortly after World War II Shusaku Endo, having graduated in French Literature from Keio University in Tokyo, was the first Japanese who went to study in France, where he devoted himself to twentieth-century French Catholic literature – the works of Muriac, Bernanos, Claudel, Maritain, *et al.* – at the University of Lyons. In those days before diplomatic relations had been re-established, the life of a lone Japanese foreign student was not altogether happy, and after three years Endo's study came to an end in serious illness. The whole experience, however, had a profound effect on his career. He learned much from the French Catholic novelists, and yet he could not escape realizing how different would be his own position in the literary world of Japan, compared to the position of Catholic men of letters operating within a Christian culture – men who had either been faithful Catholics all their lives, or men whose conversion in adult life was for them like a coming home. Endo's Catholic faith could be termed problematic, to put it politely. His favourite metaphor to describe the problem has been repeated often in his essays and public lectures: the ill-fitting suit of occidental clothes in which his mother dressed him when she had him baptized with the Christian name of Paul at the tender age of eleven years.

In the midst of his disappointment with study abroad and in the depressing circumstances of prolonged illness, Endo says that he 'came to think of becoming a novelist on my own. I felt that I had hit upon a theme peculiar to myself, which I would assume as the work of a lifetime. The theme is: To take the Christian religion which was so uncongenial to me as a Japanese, analyse why it was so uncongenial, and in some way to make it something more compatible – in other words, with my own hand I would remodel the ill-fitting suit of European clothes that my mother had dressed me in, and I would make of it a kimono more becoming to me as a Japanese.'

For Endo, as demonstrated in his writings, the quintessence of Christianity lies in God's loving compassion for His wretched children, His willingness to share with us our suffering. The Japanese heart and mind seek a merciful mother-image of God, rather than the stern, demanding, threatening father-image which (in Endo's opinion) has been unduly emphasized by the missionaries, and which accounts in great part for the failure of Christianity to strike deep roots in the 'swampland' of Japanese culture and religion. Endo is attracted to Jesus the suffering companion of all men and women, more than to Jesus the wonder-worker; he is obsessed with Jesus the human reject eventually crucified, rather than with Jesus the glorious pantocrator.

Volcano was originally published serially in 1959. Endo composed the story while he worked simultaneously on *Wonderful Fool*. This was the year immediately before the author's second prolonged hospitalization. (Hospital scenes abound in Endo's fiction.) Chronologically *Volcano* follows the early prize-winning shorter novels *White Man, Yellow Man*, and *The Sea and Poison*, and it precedes the critical and popular success of the longer novels *Silence* and *Near the Dead Sea*.

Volcano emphasizes Endo's theme of compassionate love, but in a negative way. There is pathos in the story – the problems of frustration, sickness and old age, faced by the main characters Suda and Durand – but there is no compassionate love in these two men nor in any of the other characters. *Volcano* depicts the sad state of human life when it is devoid of deep love. Suda, Ichiro, Aiba and the other non-Christians show no trace of compassion. The Christian characters, like Durand and Father Sato, go through the motions of Christian charity but without the spirit. Father Sato is satisfied with his own unanalysed and superficial piety. Durand becomes totally disillusioned in his pastoral work, then bitterly rejects the Church. Durand (who also appears in *Yellow Man*) never tires of carping about the incompatibilities between European Christianity and traditional Japanese culture and psychology. The fictional volcano of Akadaké looms over all the action as the ambivalent symbol of good and evil: Suda and Aiba fear that the mountain will erupt and destroy their self-serving schemes. Father Sato refuses to admit even the possibility of another eruption. Durand predicts that Akadaké will certainly explode and thus wipe out Father Sato's new religious retreat.

Endo has great affection for Kyushu Island and has chosen that part of Japan as the locale for many of his stories, for example the cities of Nagasaki in *Silence*, Fukuoka in *The Sea and Poison*, and Kagoshima, which is 'the city' of *Volcano*. Obviously the author found considerable material for his story in volcanology. It is reported that he even had himself lowered by helicopter into the smoking crater of Mt Sakurajima, which stands dramatically and beautifully in the Bay of Kagoshima at the southern extremity of Kyushu Island. Volcanoes fascinate the Japanese people. The mountains have been revered in tradition as manifestations of the gods. Many volcanoes are crowned with a Shinto shrine as a sacred place of pilgrimage. In modern times the craters draw hordes of tourists, many of them hikers, but many more in buses or cable-cars.

John Carroll University
Cleveland, Ohio   Richard A. Schuchert

ACKNOWLEDGEMENTS AND NOTES ON THE TRANSLATION

I am grateful to John Carroll University for continued material support in my work of translating Japanese literature. For *Volcano* in particular I must acknowledge my cross-culture debt to friends and former students: Motohisa Niiro, Masahiro Urushibata, and especially to Mrs Fumiko Ito (*née* Matsushita), who lives in Kagoshima, 'the city' of *Volcano*. These people helped me to transliterate the names of persons and places, served as interpreters for certain Japanese idioms, and translated for me into standard Japanese the Kyushu area dialect where it occurs in the original dialogue. Dr Edward J. Walter, Director of the Seismological Observatory at John Carroll University, was good enough to read the manuscript with a critical eye for technical terms relating to volcanology.

A number of Japanese words, especially many referring to household furnishings and Japanese cuisine, have no equivalent in occidental culture. Such words can be translated only by some explanatory paraphrase which tends to read awkwardly in English. I have chosen to avoid the problem and offer a glossary of Japanese words used in the text. This glossary may be found at the back of the book.

Japanese names in *Volcano* are given according to Western convention, i.e. family name last.

R.A.S.

'What a mount of heartache it is. A volcano resembles human life. In youth it gives reign to the passions, and burns with fire. It spurts out lava. But when it grows old, it assumes the burden of past evil deeds, and it turns as quiet as a grave.'

PROFESSOR KORIYAMA

ONE

The afternoon sky was clear and windless on the day which marked a festive end to the unspectacular career of Jinpei Suda. He spent the morning at his office in the Surveillance Section tidying up the odds and ends of his job. By one o'clock the men in his charge had finished their lunch break. Wreathed in smiles they returned to the office to fetch Mr Suda and conduct him, with many a pat on the back, to the third-floor assembly hall.

Outside the entrance to the hall stood a signboard with the brush-strokes of India ink still wet and shiny. It read in Japanese characters: AWARD CEREMONY FOR SECTION CHIEF SUDA. Inside the room tables were set in rows and spread with white covers. Members of the female staff moved back and forth laying out the home-made sandwiches and large-size bottles of beer.

'Suda Kun, you must be thrilled!' said Mr Sugé, Chief of the Weather Bureau, turning to greet him as he came in. The Chief was sporting a paper flower pinned to his lapel by one of the girls.

'For one thing, you have spent fifteen steady years at this weather station alone.'

Suda stood there modestly with head bowed and both hands resting on a table. His inner being did in fact overflow with emotion. It was his last day. He was leaving the Observatory which had been his post for half a lifetime. If he had cared to think about it, there had been times in the past when, unbecoming as it was to his mature years, he had entertained a certain animosity or jealousy towards the Chief, who was behind him in seniority, but who also happened to be a graduate of Tokyo

University. But on this happy occasion he gave no thought at all to any unpleasant feelings from the past.

'How about Mrs Suda? Will she be here?'

'I kept telling her to be here by one o'clock. Hasn't she arrived yet?' Suda shot a nervous look back into the corridor.

'Well anyway, let's have Suda Kun sit right here. Mrs Suda will be next to him, and let's put Aiba San and Professor Nakamura on either side of them.' Chief Sugé was giving his instructions to one of the waitresses.

'Move the vase of flowers right to the middle. The vase of flowers . . .'

He took from his pocket some notes he had written for his congratulatory speech. He put on his glasses and began to look at the notes in silence.

'I'm sorry, I'm sorry. I made the taxi speed it up, but still I'm late.'

The boisterous man who had just come in was City Councilman Aiba. He obviously had a head-start on the drinking, for he was flushed to the crown of his huge, powerful head. He wore a brilliant kimono made from the splashed pattern cloth traditional in Satsuma country. He was proprietor of the big Japanese-style inn, the Eiraku, located in the heart of the city. Rumour had it that he was elected city councilman last year with the expenditure of an enormous campaign fund.

'Well, Chief, I've just been out to lunch with Yoshioku San from the Ministry of Transportation.'

'Have you? In that case I'll ask you a favour. The Observatory this year just can't get along on the same budget as last year. With only a million and a half yen, we will have to abandon the seismological installation on Akadaké.'

'I've been pushing for it, so don't worry.'

Aiba deflected further discussion with a laugh, and turned his eye towards Suda, who stood alone in a corner of the assembly hall.

'Hello there, Suda San! This is a day for extending congratulations. But listen, there's something else I want to talk to you about.'

He winked to indicate that they should retire out into the corridor.

Suda waited in the corridor while Aiba was smiling and demonstrating his friendly feelings by patting the Chief's thin shoulders draped in a double-breasted suit. After a while he abruptly pulled away and slipped out of the room, avoiding the eyes of the others.

'The trouble, Suda, is this. We've hit a snag.' Aiba lowered his voice. 'This fellow Sasaki is still hesitating. If I can't get you to explain to him just what the situation is, then I am really stuck. How about it? Could we get together with him after this meeting?'

'What's the problem?'

Suda was nervously batting his eyes, uneasy about the Observatory Chief who was watching the two of them suspiciously.

'Sasaki is objecting that if the mountain erupts we lose it all, investment and profits alike. He still keeps talking nonsense like that. Can you please try to calm him down a little, right today?'

It had all started in the spring of this year. Section Head Suda was at work in his office at the Observatory when he received an invitation by telephone. The invitation was from Aiba, a man with whom at the time he enjoyed hardly a nodding acquaintance.

They met in the private dining-room of a restaurant located in the Hamachi district. Aiba's fat body was squeezed into an American-style suit of clothes. He kept attentively refilling Suda's cup with *sake* as he enquired whether Akadaké would ever erupt again; and in the event of another eruption, where would the danger zone be? His manner of questioning was as irritating as that of some worrisome female. As Suda heard him out, it developed that Aiba was proposing a venture to benefit the whole city. At present the little town of Shirahama, located at the foot of the volcano, held a monopoly on the tourist trade. He would run competition with Shirahama by setting up a hotel at Yokojiri, in the virgin territory lying to the north-east. He had already applied for a building permit, but he still had to enlist the support of two or three other men in the same business. In

order to sell the idea to these men he needed the help of Suda,
the scientific expert on Akadaké. It all made sense. Among the
names that Aiba offered as prospects, he included the proprietor
of the Hotel Fukuzumi, a Mr Sasaki.

After that first meeting, and after four or five more invitations
to lunch and the like, Suda came around to feeling that it might
be good to go along with Aiba. There were two secret motives
for a man in Suda's position. After his retirement from the
Weather Bureau, might there not be found an opening for him
at the new hotel? A second motive lay in his long-cherished
ambition to publish the results of his extensive research on
Akadaké. By doing a favour for Aiba, he would be putting Aiba
under obligation to himself. He could then persuade Aiba to
underwrite the cost of publication.

'I've hit a brick wall. Sasaki San is still holding out, even though
I have described the deal to him any number of times.'

Suda met Aiba's cheerless face with an expression that was
equally cheerless. It was no business frustration, however, that
bothered Suda. It was the disappointment of his own scientific
knowledge and his strongly held theory concerning Akadaké
being rejected.

'So I am asking you, this afternoon, if you have the time,
please come with Sasaki Kun and me for an on-the-spot look.
Otherwise we will never convince him.'

The Award Ceremony scheduled for one o'clock finally got
started by nearly two. First of all, Observatory Chief Sugé
placed his notes on the lectern and began the formal introduction
of Suda, who was now seated along with his wife. The Chief
drew a sketch of Jinpei Suda's career: how he had laboured
for the Meteorological Station at Dairen, in the Province of
Kwantung (Manchuria), for nearly twenty years, transferring
after that to the present Observatory where he served as head
of the Surveillance Section; how as an executive he had won
the affectionate respect of his staff; how in official responsibili-
ties Sugé himself remained the ranking officer, but yet how
often it had happened that even the Chief had been saved by
Suda's accurate predictions on the region's weather; and deserving of special mention were his painstaking observations on

Akadaké. Sugé's speech went on and on, generously larded with technical terms borrowed from his expert knowledge of German.

'It should be noted that Suda San is the gentleman whom we nicknamed the "Akadaké Demon".' When the Chief directed a mildly derisive smile in Suda's direction, a brief outbreak of laughter and a smattering of applause came from the younger men at the back tables.

'As you can understand from that clapping just now, they tell me that since he took office here the Akadaké Demon has climbed that mountain actually in excess of eighty times. At present, however, because he has grown old in service, our younger staff members have taken over responsibility for field observations. Nevertheless, in the entire length and breadth of Japan there is no equal to Suda San when it comes to Akadaké. At the Observatory here we know that for a fact.'

Seen through the window, the top of the volcano was hidden in a cloud bank. The mountain lay on the other side of a peaceful bay. It was about two and a half miles from the city. In spite of the luminous afternoon sunshine, the mountain itself appeared in a misty purple light. Even that mountain has grown old, thought Suda, as he stole a sideways glance at his wife Taka. Her face was sallow from a weak stomach. She sat quietly, hands in her lap, eyes closed, listening to the speech of Chief Sugé.

Next to speak was City Councilman Aiba, and in his characteristic strong voice he yammered on and on about how his personal relationship with Mr Suda had more recently bloomed into intimate friendship; how the fact that they possessed so eminent a person as this in the city's Weather Bureau was a point of distinction not only for the Bureau itself, but was in truth a high honour for the whole civic community.

About the time that the younger staff members had annihilated the sandwiches, and only a few half-finished bottles of beer and pop remained on the tables, Chief Sugé got around to presenting the formal testimonial plaque memorializing fifteen years of continuous service. With the plaque went a commemorative flower vase. Bathed in applause from the whole assembly,

Suda was holding up the cumbersome, solid flower vase when all of a sudden he felt dizzy. The face of the Chief went out of focus, as though he was seeing it through a layer of film. His legs wobbled, but Suda exerted self-control enough to get back to his seat, and in a few moments the vertigo went away. So it was that at some time after three o'clock the meeting came to an end.

Letting Aiba and Taka wait for him at the main entrance, Suda returned once more to his office. The young men, like Kato and Kinoshita and the others, were already back at work after leaving the assembly hall. Raising his hand in a gesture to prevent their standing up, Suda disappeared behind the screen that enclosed his old cubicle. He sat down at the desk, which had already been tidied up and even polished by one of the office girls. Nothing remained of his personal effects. Once more he inspected the now empty drawers, feeling keenly the prospect that from tomorrow on he would never face that desk again. He realized that Aiba and his wife would get tired of waiting for him, but he just wanted to sit there quietly for a few moments. Blinking his eyes while lighting a cigarette, he caught sight of Akadaké through the window. He gazed at the mountain listlessly. He was the man who was always looking at the volcano from this very spot in this same position at the desk. A little while ago the Observatory Chief had referred to him as the Akadaké Demon, but the Chief was wrong. Suda had been in his mid-forties when he came from Dairen to assume his post here. Immediately he had set about coming to grips with the true character of Akadaké. He could not avoid being nicknamed the Demon, at that time. But now he had swung around to where he no longer felt any drive to fight the mountain. That earlier, scrappy attitude had matured to a peaceful feeling of affection for the aged mountain. So it seemed. In the last year or so, Suda had begun to realize that just as he himself had grown old, so Akadaké had become utterly decrepit compared to what it had been fifteen years before.

Akadaké is a volcano that rises to 6,000 feet above sea level. Its reputation goes back to antiquity. In the Mesozoic era of geological history, under the influence of the related volcanic

activity of Daisen and Sanbe mountains, together with the volcanic chain of Yufu, Tsurumi and the Juju cluster, there occurred
in the zone of Akadaké a topographical cave-in which produced
a caldera. Sea water engulfed the caldera cavity, thus originating
the broad bight which now spreads out from the city like a
reflecting mirror. Akadaké is said to be the result of an elevation
formed around a wide volcanic fissure which broken open at a
point overlooking the south-east area of the bay. The ground-
level foundation of the volcanic knoll bellied up, and the fissure
disgorged its rock-forming materials, giving rise to the present-
day three craggy eminences of Akadaké: South Peak, Middle
Peak, and North Peak.

In historical times there have been a number of notable eruptions. Even in the most ancient annals, those for the Sixth Year
of the Emperor Tenmu (AD 678?), that is, 'in the winter Tenth
Month of the Year of the Tiger occurring in the Fifth Order of
the Sexagenary Cycle', it is written:

> Disastrous conflagration. Sandy gravel waste piles up. Moun-
> tain roars like giant drums. Ashes fall like rain. All vegetation
> withers.

The ancient record is terse, but it does describe the pattern of
a violent eruption. Since then, and down through history to the
time of the Emperor Meiji (AD 1866–1912), Akadaké belched
fire, rained ashes, and brought earthquakes to the villages
below. But among all the eruptions the ones that have remained
fixed in people's memories, even today, are the great eruption
in the Eighth Year of Emperor Bunmei (AD 1476) and another
in the Seventeenth Year of Emperor Meiji (AD 1882).

> The mountain flares up stupendously. Since five days ago the
> water from wells near the beach explodes like geysers, and
> the sea water turns purple. Continuously up to the ninth day
> of the Tenth Month, from Akadaké a white smoke shoots
> out, but from the area above the village of Arimura comes a
> great belching of black smoke. The smoke rises in the sky
> to a height of more than seven miles. Inside the smoke cloud

the volcano flashes innumerable bolts of lightning. It spews skyward glowing coals, which fall on the island, burning completely 161 houses on contact. By the next day, the tenth, from the Hour of the Hare [6 am–8 am], even though the rain of glowing coals stops, in its place fall gritty ashes, followed by tons of muddy mire piling to a depth of three or four feet on the farms in the bottom land and to a depth of nearly a foot on the mountain slopes. Most notably on the west side the release of lava inundates the villages, covers the paddy fields, and flows into the sea. The sound, which was originally forty fathoms deep, is gradually filled in.

This is an excerpt from the *Record of Natural Disasters*, describing conditions in the Eighth Year of Bunmei. But the eruption in the Seventeenth Year of Meiji was even more violent. The Tokyo *Nichi-Nichi* newspaper at that time carried the following account:

At about 8 am January 12 the top of Akadaké belched intermittently bun-shaped puffs of white smoke. Eventually around 10 am came the explosion, at first from the west flank of the mountain at an elevation of 2,850 feet, followed not 10 minutes later by an explosion from an elevation of about 3,200 feet on the south-east flank. In the windless atmospheric conditions prevailing at the time, the smoke rose straight up to a height of nearly 20,000 feet. The mountain touched off a long cannonade of lightning flashes within the dense smoke, with the roar of violent detonations. Then came the final grand eruption accompanied with incessant earthquakes and the booming of thunder.

What came next was an enormous flow of lava, a full kilometre wide and nearly fifty metres deep. At first the river of lava rolled down the sloping reaches of the mountain at a speed of 200 metres per hour. But the width of the flow gradually expanded as it stretched for the sea, and it completely covered the villages of Yokoyama and Uda on the south-east corner of the island.

The lava pushed into the sea to a distance of nearly 3,500 yards. Furthermore, the lava flow on the south-east side completely buried a hill of some 300-foot elevation and extended the seacoast to a distance of some 1,400 yards.

After the Meiji Era, however, and therefore during the fifteen years since Suda had arrived on the scene, Akadaké had never caused any catastrophe, and in fact had never again erupted. At most, in the year after Suda came to town Akadaké had begun oddly enough to raise a plume of thin smoke from the very top, contrary to its previous history when it had always found its point of fissure at some fragile spot on the sloping sides. After an investigation by Kyoto University's Dr Koriyama it was understood that the white smoke was not a warning sign of further eruption. Quite the contrary, it was a sign that Akadaké had gradually changed from an active volcano into a dormant volcano. Observing this mountain's character, the learned man theorized that in its period of greatest activity the explosions had come from the lower reaches of the mountainside. Then step by step the eruptions moved to higher positions where their force gradually abated. The fact that Akadaké now raised some smoke from its very top only proved that the mountain was approaching its day of death as a volcano. In short, Akadaké was stricken with old age.

Until taking up his duties here, Jinpei Suda had no particular interest in volcanoes. During those twenty years at the weather station in Dairen his job lay rather in plotting the course of typhoons and in keeping track of routine barometric readings. But in the year after his transfer he became associated with Dr Koriyama's research team, and he learned for the first time what kind of mountain a volcano really was. Being a man of integrity, Suda immersed himself in the study of rock reading, lava analysis and seismology. He showed more enthusiasm than the university students in the party. Dr Koriyama had remarked that 'a volcano by its nature is a living being'. Suda was magnetized. He was not himself a university graduate, but in his humble position of staff member in the Surveillance Section the challenge of trying to come to grips with Akadaké became the mainspring of his life.

Suda crushed his half-smoked cigarette in the ashtray and stepped over to the window. He saw the white-painted excursion boat moving slowly over the bay as it always did. A bank of purple-edged clouds concealed the upper half of the volcano, but the sun had descended far enough to illuminate the area around the Sixth Station on the mountain heights. The ugly furrows in the mountain surface – like the wrinkles in an elephant hide – stood out in high relief.

From the aged volcano Suda's thoughts turned abruptly to his own prospects. After leaving the Weather Bureau he might find an opening at the new hotel, thanks to Aiba. But such a position would likely involve duties of no concern to a man who until today had spent his time wrestling with Akadaké. What he wanted to do was to write up his observations of the mountain. After Dr Koriyama's death there had been no one but Suda to collect detailed data on the change of Akadaké from active volcano to dormant. He wanted to leave the material behind in permanent form of one kind or another. He kept blinking his eyes as he thought how the mountain, now grown old and emitting only thin vapour, was somehow like himself.

'Shall I pay old Akadaké a visit today? It has been quite a while since the last.'

He recalled what Aiba had suggested earlier, about the favour of taking Sasaki to show him around the mountain. He had completely forgotten that Aiba and Mrs Suda were waiting for him at the front entrance.

After once more extending farewells to the underlings in the Surveillance Section, he went downstairs. His wife Taka was seated on a bench, holding in her lap the flower vase wrapped in a decorative kerchief. There was no sign of Aiba, not even in the sunlit courtyard.

'Well, Taka, how about you? What are your plans for the afternoon?' Suda was speaking while he slipped an arm into his ancient all-weather topcoat. 'I'm thinking of going over to the island for a little, with Aiba and another man. Will you come along?'

His wife gave him a startled look but didn't answer.

'Are you coming or not?'

'You know perfectly well. It's my heart condition. I can't go up on those mountain roads.'

Suda nodded his head with a grunt. 'All right, then just take the vase and the plaque along home with you. How about Aiba? Where did he disappear to?'

Approaching the little harbour of Shirahama, the starboard side of the excursion boat rode close to the jagged rocks along the water's edge which formed a natural breakwater to protect the bluff. These rocks were fragments from the lava flow dating back to the Bunmei Era. Although a stream of lava will normally slow down as it reaches level ground, it is reported that at the time there were some simple-minded serfs who leaped into the sea ahead of it and drowned.

At this time the lava zone was government property. Land was for sale at only seven yen per *tsubo*, but there had been no takers. The area had neither gas nor water pipes. The town of Shirahama operated a sightseeing aquarium standing on the lava bed, where the dazzling sun-darts bouncing from the surface of the sea danced along the building's concrete wall. The refreshment parlours and souvenir shops which came into view employed a scratchy loudspeaker system to broadcast a popular song. The guides holding up their official pennants and the bus conductor girls in uniform were lined up just off the landing pier, waiting for the passengers.

Suda was jammed between the obese Aiba on one side and Sasaki on the other as the crowd of passengers pushed off into the blinding ultra-violet sunlight of the pier. The light was so painfully brilliant that he had to keep his eyes squinted shut even when somebody stopped him to say hello.

'Well, well, so you've brought the Councilman along with you this time! How've you been? We haven't seen you here for quite a while.'

The little man dressed up in business suit and canvas shoes was the proprietor of one of the refreshment parlours.

'We've just finished the Award Ceremony. I expect you heard

about it, it was in the morning paper. Suda San was cited by the Ministry of Transportation for his fifteen years of service.' Aiba anticipated Suda and explained the circumstances as he tap-tapped his *geta* to dislodge a stone stuck between the cleats.

When other patrons in the pavilion abruptly turned to gaze at Suda with eyes of curiosity and respect, Suda felt mildly elated.

'What are your plans for the rest of the day?'

'We're going as far as Point Shimoné on some business.'

'The weather is nice. I hope you enjoy it.'

When they walked into the waiting-room of the bus terminal, again a number of acquaintances offered greetings to the three of them. But unlike all the rest, Suda was something special, for whenever he went out to survey Akadaké he could ride free on the boat and on the bus.

'Who's driving on the next bus?' In his painfully jovial manner Aiba was joshing the young lady tour-guide.

'Who did you say? Young Kimura? If he's the driver and you're the conductor, I'd better take out some insurance!'

But in sharp contrast to Aiba's high spirits the third member of the party, Mr Sasaki, kept rubbing his chin with his right hand. He looked ill at ease and remained silent. Suda gathered from his expression that Sasaki had no heart whatsoever for Aiba's scheme.

When the bus had left the town, it raised a cloud of dust along the country road closed in on either side by extensive orchards. Growing on the slopes near the foot of the mountain were the island's famous product, tangerines. The fruit was ready for picking. The ashy volcanic soil grew nothing but tangerines, and some patches of giant radishes and peanuts. The little town of Shirahama with its monopoly on the tourist business was an exception, but the back country hamlets were poverty-stricken and wretched. Farmhouses were caked with volcanic ash and dust, low-slung and unsanitary like pig-sties. Barefoot women walking along the road carried baskets on their heads. And not only the women. Children coming home from school put their book bags on their heads. Most of them were barefoot too. Supporting one's pack on the head was the custom on the island. It made things easier on the narrow mountain paths.

At one hamlet after another the bus gradually discharged passengers with their loads of fish and vegetables, until there were left near the back only Suda's party and three young men who seemed to be college boys. The bus was challenging an especially steep hill, and the wheels squeaked on the pumice stone every time they negotiated one of the hairpin turns.

The trio of Suda, Aiba and Sasaki got off as planned at bleak and chilly Point Shimoné, located at the Third Station level. The pale sunlight of late afternoon fell on the copses. Without a word the three of them started walking up the mountain road cluttered with chunks of lava, rock cinders, gritty pumice. To their left lay a bluff, reddish near the bottom but changing to a liver-colour towards the top. Suda had travelled all over this mountain for fifteen years and could tell at a glance by just which eruption any particular stratum had been laid down. He explained the phenomena to Aiba and Sasaki as they walked along. Aiba reacted with extravagant expressions of deferential esteem for the expertise of Jinpei Suda. Sasaki as ever said nothing.

The down slope to their right was overgrown with stunted thickets and ground-creeping shrubs. The reddish-looking trees standing here and there were sumac. Except for the occasional sumac there were no other trees to display the blazing tints of autumn leaves, even though it was that time of year. The subterranean heat of the volcano discouraged the growth of trees.

From over the rim of the scarp Akadaké displayed her full aspect. The sky appeared clear when they looked up at it from Shirahama, but from their present elevation a cloud bank covered the top of the mountain. With the sun's decline the clouds were less brilliant, yet here and there the cloud bank broke, and rays of evening light fanned out to touch the western reaches of the solemn mountain, causing its ugly grey corrugations to stand out in high relief. As far up as the Sixth Station level the mountain was covered with yellowish overgrowth, broken here and there with patches of blackish lava, the burnt out areas from an ancient eruption.

'If you go up ahead there just a bit, you get a view of what's left of a big lava flow. But I'm all out of breath.' Aiba was mumbling to Sasaki. He was not only grossly overweight, but he was wearing elevated wooden clogs. 'I'll just wait for you here. You two please go ahead.' Aiba was panting hard.

'It's only a little further. Try and come on.'

Proceeding up the mountain road, Suda was gratified at his own good physical condition for a man of fifty-nine years, in contrast to Aiba, who had to plunk himself down on a smooth volcanic boulder after walking only another hundred feet.

'Suda San. Let's stop here.'

Sasaki kept his skinny back towards Aiba as he looked up at the mountain. His sallow complexion betrayed a bilious stomach. He hawked up a greenish oyster of phlegm and let it fly at the lava in front of him. Then in a tone of voice calculated to humour Sasaki, Suda said to him. 'You must be pretty tired yourself. In general that's the location I recommend, from the ridge of this hill in front of us and from there on down the slope.'

'The view isn't very good,' Sasaki answered in a low voice.

'From here it's not so good, you're right, but shall we take a look from the crest of the hill? Because from there you get the night view of the city lights as well as a bird's-eye view of Shirahama, Wari-ishi-zaki and the inlet at Matsu-ura. But our first consideration must be the water supply and public transportation, and so this is far and away the best location.'

'If the site is too near the crater, or if there is an earthquake, it's dangerous and it won't do.'

'But the ground is solid.'

With a foxy glint in his eye Aiba turned to look at Suda.

'Suda San! Please explain to Sasaki Kun how it has always been with eruptions on Akadaké. To judge from the way he's talking now, he must be waiting to hear what the expert has to say.'

Looking at the volcanic stones lying in the road, Suda selected one, picked it up, and launched again into the very practical, non-technical explanation which he had given so many times before.

'The depression you see over in that direction is generally considered to be the source of the eruption back in the Keicho

Era. If you ask how we know that, well, we can judge from the age of the rocks. But even clearer evidence is provided by the elevation of the crater, about 350 metres above sea level.'

Then he raised a finger and pointed up towards the barren surface of Akadaké, visible now in the pale glow of evening. He was indicating what remained of a stream of black lava which ran along like a thread laid out on the mountainside.

'That dates back to the Bunmei Era. It's way over 800 metres high. Over on the right, do you see the big hole shaped like a horse's eye? That's the location of the explosion during the Meiji Era. From all these indications we gather that the recurrent eruptions of Akadaké moved up each time to a higher and higher elevation. Never once has an eruption occurred at a place lower than any of the previous eruptions.'

'Why is that?'

'Well, we can't really say. Even in the world of science there are several different hypotheses, but we admit that we don't yet understand the cause. At any rate, following the highly regarded word of Professor Koriyama, Akadaké is said to be an upward-moving type of volcano.'

Sasaki as usual said nothing and kept rubbing his chin with his right hand. The silence, and the deeply skeptical expression, seemed to Suda like contempt for Koriyama. And they wounded his own feelings of personal pride.

Of course he had come here with Aiba and this man out of self-serving interest for his own future. If he could put Aiba under obligation to himself, then Aiba would make it possible to publish the record of his fifteen years of data-gathering on Akadaké.

But even more than that, it was intolerable to Suda that Sasaki was not at all inclined to accept his theory and his firm conviction that this volcano was already in process of extinction. The basis of Suda's self-assurance was a secret vanity born of the fact that he himself was the only man in the whole Japanese Meteorological Service to make any on-the-spot field observations to support the late Dr Koriyama's theory.

The sun began to set. It was getting a little chilly. Aiba and Sasaki stood in the road discussing the lie of the land. Aiba

prattled on in his loud voice as he drew a circle on the ground
with the end of a dry stick.

Jinpei Suda left the two men and went off by himself up the
incline rising to the left. In the desolate evening light Akadaké
exposed for him the expanse of her naked skin with its ugly
greyish wrinkles. The sight was forlorn, solitary. Yet this was
the mountain that in ages past had spouted fire to the heavens
above, spewed up stones, released an overwhelming stream of
lava. From the place that Suda had pointed out to Sasaki, the
black river had flowed as much as a kilometre wide and fifty
metres deep, running down on Hiki-no-hira, pushing over the
level surface below, submerging villages on the shoreline.

In the last twelve or thirteen years, Suda had set foot in that
lava zone any number of times. The first time was when he
explored with the late Dr Koriyama and his students from Kyoto
University. Suda was then in his forties, in the vigorous prime
of life. Sometimes he had been out in front of the students. At
other times he had carried the Doctor's equipment. High above
the expedition a flock of birds would wheel and turn through
the overcast sky in search of food. Then on the spur of the
moment Dr Koriyama had murmured some words, and now on
the spur of the moment Suda recalled the words.

'What a mount of heartache it is. A volcano resembles human
life. In youth it gives rein to passions, and burns with fire. It
spurts out lava. But when it grows old, it assumes the burden
of those past evil deeds, and it turns quiet as a grave. You
younger men can hardly fathom the pathos of this mountain.'

The students giggled good-humouredly. Even Suda at that
time, being what he was, took the remark as just another one of
those sententious observations that are characteristic of learned
men. But now, after Suda had played out his own role in life,
his reaction was quite different. The Professor's low-toned mur-
murings rode on the chilly breeze blowing down from the slope.
Suda felt the breeze penetrating body and soul.

Until recently Suda had not been much given to serious
reflection on his own life, or to any brooding over the past.
If he gave it any thought at all, he found nothing particularly

singular. Like the common run of men he accepted life on its own terms, meeting each day as it came along.

Both at the Weather Bureau and at the local Observatory he worked so steadily and in such dead earnest that his colleagues considered him a grind. From the time he had arrived in this city he had no other hobby worthy of the name beyond his relentless tussle with Akadaké. By way of exception perhaps once a month he went to the house of a friend for a game of *go*.

Of course in his youth he had sowed his wild oats like anybody else. He had suffered a bit of woman trouble. But after he married his wife Taka he was well aware how dangerous it was to depart from the social controls imposed on his career and on his private life. From fifty years of experience in the art of getting along in the world, he had learned that mediocrity was the secret of contentment.

So even as he reached retirement today, and was leaving the place where he'd worked for half a lifetime, there was no particular failure nor any unhappy memory to cause him regret. He had achieved nothing spectacular, but by the same token he felt that he had never made any mistake that would merit the finger of scorn from others. During the Award Ceremony this secret sense of satisfaction had filled his heart. But when he stood there now, face to face with Akadaké in the dusk, an unexplainable melancholy swept over him. Stuffing his hands into the pockets of his shabby weatherall coat, Suda thought of his feeling as a sign of old age. He thought of how a man loses courage as he takes on years.

Just at the moment he bestirred himself to move on, he suddenly felt another attack of dizziness. He pressed one hand against his forehead, waiting stock-still until the bothersome light-headed feeling would depart.

The same kind of vertigo had hit him during the Award Ceremony, at the moment he reached out to accept the flower vase from the Observatory Chief. 'I was all tired out from cleaning out my desk and from the excitement of the party,' he thought. He squatted down on the cold pumice stone waiting for the vertigo to subside.

Then somehow or other there crossed his mind the memory

of a certain evening during the previous week. It was one of those nights when he got home late from the Observatory.

His oldest son Ichiro had not yet returned from work at the Company. He learned that his daughter-in-law Sakiko was also away, on the plea of having some business at the home of a friend.

'Really you can't depend on these young women nowadays. While their husbands are out working, the wives themselves are always off somewhere.'

His wife Taka was grumbling as she served the meal at the table set just for the two of them. Suda plied his chopsticks in silence.

'Did you hear, Pess from next door was dead after all. In the woods on Mt Shirayama. That's where the neighbour's kids found his carcass.'

Aware that Suda was paying no attention at all, Taka mumbled on as though talking to herself.

'Do you suppose a dog senses when it's going to die?'

That night, Suda happened to wake up again. It was becoming more frequent for him to wake in the middle of the night. And then he would have a hard time getting back to sleep.

He slid the tray of smoking accessories close to the bedding and smoked a cigarette. On the floor-bed next to him Taka was snoring noisily. When he reached out a hand to stop her snoring, he recalled a book he had once read just to kill some time. The book had said it was hard for an old man, since the only time he used his hands to touch the body of his wife in bed was when he tried to stop her from snoring. In the darkness Suda all of a sudden remembered the dog Pess that Taka had been telling him about. Maybe that old dog had hidden out in the woods because he had felt a premonition of death. Rubbing his scalp with his fingers he thought, for the first time as it were, of how the only things lying ahead of him were old age and death. That evening and that night all alone with Taka – these were the things that Suda recalled, squatting down on the cold pumice stones.

TWO

The reputation of Father Ginzo Sato was by no means unde-served. The young seminarians in the diocese liked him for being a jovial sort of fellow and something of a philistine. The laity recognized him as a man not unacquainted with the world as many a priest is apt to be unacquainted. He was aware of the sweetness and the bitterness of life, and people considered him a good talker.

Unlike some of those priests up in Tokyo, Father Sato had no taste for the concise reasoning involved in problematical theological discussions. Being the only priest in his part of the city, he did a lot more than offer Mass at the church. Of late, as time permitted, he would take the mini-car which he had learned to drive, and off he would go to make the rounds of Catholic homes or to visit the sick. He was prepared to listen to everybody's hard-luck story. He had occasion to speak with young students when they came to the church, and he would assume an attitude worthy of the students. He never neglected to recite for their benefit selections from a poem which he had read in the seminary many years before. It was Kenji Miyazawa's famous *Amé ni mo Maké-zu* ('Undaunted by the Rain').

> Watch closely, listen carefully,
> Learn everything you can,
> Counting ne'er the cost to self.
> Be there a sick child in the East,
> Go and nurse him well.
> Be there a mother in the West,
> Go and hoist her bale.

Then with a good-natured smile on his healthy round face he
would ask: 'This inclination of the heart, isn't it really like St
Francis of Assisi? Here is a Japanese, ignorant of the teachings
of Christianity, yet he is able to enter into the same spirit of
faith as St Francis.'

At the Catholic church in Kurata-cho, where Father Sato
served as pastor, Mass began every Sunday at eight o'clock in
the morning. The chapel was a room of less than 300 square
feet, laid out with *tatami*. A score or more of the Christians
were always in place by 7.30, some of them kneeling on the
tatami, some of them squatting, but all waiting patiently for the
altar candles to be lit. Men took their places on the right, with
the women in their white veils on the left. Father would soon
appear at the altar with his fat frame squeezed into the sacred
vestments. Through all those minutes before Mass the air was
charged with the dissonance of coughing spells, the blowing of
noses, and the susuration of mothers scolding their tots for
being restless. The schoolgirls were on the floor in a group
around the organ, piously hugging song books to their bosoms
and taking care not to expose their legs.

In contrast to the practice in Protestant worship, at a Catholic
Mass the priest does not necessarily deliver a sermon for the
faithful. Normally sermons are limited to Sunday and the major
Feast Days of the Church.

Today was a Sunday, but before Father Ginzo Sato launched
into the homily he had prepared the night before, he put a smile
on his face and started off with something else.

'As you all well know,' he said, 'this Sunday happens to fall
on the day when the Catholic Church celebrates the Feast of
the Blessed Mother's Presentation in the Temple. But before
that, let me tell you a piece of good news.'

Father Sato knew the individual faces of all the Christians
squatting in front of him, all on their best behaviour, hands
resting on their knees. He knew them through and through –
the old Christians, of course; but even the new converts were
people whom he had taken in hand for catechetical instruction
and led to the ceremony of baptism. In the middle of the front
row sat a young housewife, Teruko Nosawa, looking forlorn

and with her eyes downcast. The priest knew that Teruko's mother-in-law had been making trouble since Teruko had become a Catholic. And over near one of the pillars Father saw a man who was shifting his weight to relieve the numbness in his legs caused by sitting too long on his heels. He was a white-collar employee in one of the big conglomerates, a man who had worked hard over many years to support his oldest son, a helpless victim of polio. Father Sato understood these sad situations from first-hand experience. He himself had grown up on one of those not very prosperous farms in the Goto Islands off the coast of Kyushu. He could see in the faces of his Christians that attitude towards life peculiar to their class in society – the social class to which he himself had been born. He knew the joys and sorrows that were theirs. He was unfailingly aware that he had no right to be too severe while directing these men and women in their religious duties.

'The news touches something that I have been discussing with you for a long time. It concerns the retreat house, St Theresa's Villa. At last the way has been cleared to making the retreat house a reality.'

The priest looked around the chapel, savouring the reaction of the congregation. It was then that he took note of a student near the front whose face he did not recognize, but the boy was hanging on every word he said, just like the others in church. His neck was whitish and thin like a chicken's, sticking out from the military collar of his student uniform. His eyes nictated nervously behind his glasses. 'He's probably non-Christian,' thought Father Sato. Around that particular period there were a number of students from the new-system university in town who occasionally took a look into the church, moved by curiosity or by a short-lived interest in the search for religious truth. So the appearance of another young man of the type was nothing new.

'At first the Bishop opposed the whole idea, but he came to realize the zeal of Horita San and Kuki San and other members of the committee, and now he even feels favourable to helping us financially. Once we solve the money problem, I would like to acquire a piece of land near the foot of Akadaké at a spot a little above the village of Wari-ishi-zaki.'

The lot in Kurata-cho on which the Catholic church stood was very small. There was no room to put a kindergarten for the children, nor a club house for the young men. Still, what the Christians needed most was a place where perhaps once a year they could leave behind the cares of the world and devote themselves completely to the life of faith. This was the long-felt desire of Father Ginzo Sato. He had been a parish priest for nearly thirty years. He understood completely the situation of the men and women facing him, how, overwhelmed as they were with their daily routine, they could not always carry out their religious duties, and they could not pray as Christians really should. For the clergy there were places like monasteries where several times a year a priest could withdraw for silent meditation on his union with God. Was it not, therefore, even more urgent to establish a holy place for the ordinary lay people living in their profane environment?

'I realize that all of you are faithful in religious practice. Our average attendance at Mass is splendid. There are more parents sending their children to catechism class. These are facts. Nevertheless, as long as we live in this world, it often happens that our souls are stained with the wickedness of the world. It will be good for us once a year to forsake the world and all our occasions of sin, and to spend a few days at this peaceful mountain villa.'

The faces of the Christians were a marvel to behold. Even the student whom Father didn't know kept batting his eyes and looking directly up at the priest. Father Sato smiled and made a deep bow to acknowledge the favourable reception of his remarks.

The sermon came next, after which the ritual of the Mass took up where it had left off. When the chancel bell sounded for Holy Communion, almost everyone moved up to kneel in front of the altar. Just as Father had conceded, the people of his parish were good observers of the teachings of the Church. Father Sato moved along the row of kneeling Christians, hovering for a moment over every upturned head with its slightly sunken cheeks and wistful countenance. He placed a white particle of bread from the ciboriun into the mouth of every one of them.

At the end he turned to the people, spread his arms, and intoned with a loud voice the Latin formula of dismissal: *'Ite, missa est.'*

The desiccated organ finished off a final hymn, and the Christians felt a sense of reprieve as they headed for the vestibule, raising a clattering racket near the footgear lockers, then moving along to the Sunday outside. The chapel inside was quiet, though it still retained the odour of stirred up dust. Father Sato removed his Mass vestments in the sacristy and then returned to the chapel. He saw the unfamiliar student standing near one of the pillars, left there all by himself with his white, tense face.

'I suppose this is the first time you have attended Mass.'

When Father came near in his affable manner, the student blinked excitedly behind his thickset glasses.

'No, Father, I've been a Catholic since I was little.' Then he said in a low voice, 'Uh . . . , can you please hear my confession?'

'Confession is it?' Father Sato nodded. 'Yes, of course. But why don't you go to confession in your own parish?'

The boy was tongue-tied, and Father got the point immediately. From long years of experience he was well acquainted with the psychology of a Catholic in this situation. Because the pastor of his own church knows him so well and will recognize him in confession, a Catholic can feel ashamed to reveal his sins. It's a hard thing to do, so he goes quietly to another parish for confession.

'Let's use the confessional. And how about the prayers before confession, have you been through them already?'

'Yes, Father.'

The confessional was a hushed narrow cubicle near the entrance. Except for a wooden crucifix hanging in full view on the wall there was no trace of any other ornamentation. A metal screen partition faces the penitent as he kneels on the *prie-dieu,* and behind the screen sits the priest, supporting his forehead on one hand to incline his ear to the penitent.

After a mechanical recitation of the opening formula, the student began his confession. 'I . . . , I uhh . . .' His voice was thick and the next words wouldn't come out.

'What's the matter? Please go on.'

'Since my last confession three months ago, a girl, that is my cousin and I . . .'

Father kept listening in silence. He heard an audible gulp when the student swallowed hard in his distress.

'You committed a sin of the flesh, is that it? Is this girl a Christian?'

'No.'

'How many times?'

'What?'

'How many? I mean how many times did you do it?'

'It was . . . just once.'

Through a window came the shrill voices of the children playing with a skipping rope in the churchyard. Father Sato sighed.

'It was really just the once, was it?'

'Yes, Father.'

In his heart Father felt relieved. He wiped some perspiration from his forehead. The boy's curdled voice seemed to indicate that he felt bad about what he had done. Fornication is a mortal sin, but because the student had come forward of his own accord to confess the shameful deed, Father had to give him credit for his courage and his strength of character.

'Any other sins?'

In a low voice the student mumbled two or three other misdeeds, but they were nothing of moment. In the language of the Church these were known as venial sins. Through the metal screen Father Sato delivered his strict admonition: that human beings are weak, but they must use their will power to triumph over sin; that the boy must avoid any occasion where he might be in danger of touching his cousin again.

'For your penance say the Lord's Prayer twenty times.'

The 'penance' for sins that Father Sato imposed on the Christians was always lenient and easy to perform. To reveal one's shameful sins is torturesome. In Father's opinion this act of courageous will power was usually penance enough.

Father pronounced the formula of absolution in the usual way, but even so the student remained there motionless. Then he did raise himself halfway from the *prie-dieu*, but with eyes blinking furiously behind the glasses he settled down again to his knees.

'Go in peace now.'

Behind the metal screen Father Sato had a quizzical look on his face as he tried to excuse the penitent.

'I just can't,' said the student weakly.

'What's the trouble?'

'No matter how often I go to confession, it doesn't do any good. Lately it's got so I don't even know whether I'm making a good confession.'

'Why not?'

'Saying a prayer ten times or so . . . is that really enough to be forgiven for what I did?'

'I gave you sacramental absolution, didn't I? Jesus Himself takes on the burden of your sins when He acts through me. You know that.'

'Father . . .' The student was pressing close to the screen, and his fetid breath blew directly into the face of the priest. 'I never feel sorry for anything I do. Even when I had intercourse with my cousin, I didn't have a bad conscience. I never felt dirty. Why not? If I was worried at all, it was only because somebody else might find out what we did. So even now I don't feel sure . . .'

The student's foul breath was like pyorrhoea. Father Sato averted his face a little to avoid it. He gave a sigh of relief. The penitent's scruples were a phenomenon occurring often enough with young people, even with seminarians. They were inclined to be excessively hard on themselves. From his long experience he also realized that extreme self-torture of this kind did not necessarily lead to any mature development of faith or of human personality.

'It is written in the Bible, "Unless ye become as little children . . . ,"' said the priest, launching into a fervorino for the jittery student's benefit. He explained how we must accept the teachings of the faith in a spirit of humility and simplicity, like little children.

The ministry of a priest is much like the work of a physician involved with the painful maladies of his clients. Just as the physician will remonstrate with a patient excessively perturbed about his ailments, so Father Sato diagnosed the anxiety of the student as nothing more than the imbalance of youth. In reality Father Sato had no insight whatsoever into the young man's psychology, because he himself had never in his life experienced any doubt in his personal faith nor any frustration with the precepts of the Church.

'When St Theresa's Villa is ready for use, in the pleasant surroundings of nature, even you will learn to be humble.' Exasperation now tinged the voice of the priest admonishing the student who looked up at him.

Father Sato had recently been trying to make his pastoral visits to the homes of the newly baptized Christians on Sundays, after a late breakfast. This particular Sunday was followed immediately by Labour Thanksgiving Day, a national holiday. The city's main street was bustling with people, and Shirayama Park was filled with family groups out to enjoy the warm autumn sun in the leisure of the long weekend. The town had been almost completely burned out by an air raid during the war. It was now bereft of any signs of having been an historical castle town. But thanks to the air raid, the city had been able to lay out some very wide streets. There were no high buildings like a big metropolis, and even the number of taxis cruising about were few. It looked like the citizens enjoyed more of these wide avenues than they could really make use of. Behind Shirayama Park there stood an enormous public housing project erected by the Prefectural government. This housing complex had become the new number one showplace of the city. Father Sato was going to visit a Christian by the name of Shinoda, who lived in one of these apartments.

The number of Christians had been growing for two or three years. Right after the war many groups of young people had come for a look at the church, attracted by the novelty of Christianity or motivated by a kind of restless curiosity, but after a while they disappeared. The recent converts, however, were a more sober sort, and for that very reason they were more reliable. The Christian named Shinoda had received baptism sometime during the long period he was confined in the Tuberculosis Sanitorium. He was a white-collar worker, a serious man and very fervent.

Father Sato purchased a bag of caramels near the Park as a gift for the Shinoda's little boy, who was attending catechism classes on Saturday afternoons in preparation for First Communion.

It was only a two-room apartment, one room with six *tatami* and the other with four. Mrs Shinoda had decorated one of the walls with a colour print of the Madonna, and she had even arranged a little altar fitting into the *tokonoma*, which served as a focal point for family prayer. Father Sato was not at all displeased when he observed these signs.

After an hour of chatting about pleasantries he left the Shinodas' apartment. The sky was beginning to shade off with the approach of evening. Beyond the town Akadaké was wrapped in a purple cloud. A loudspeaker in Shirayama Park was blaring out some trashy popular song. Little by little the family groups were beginning to head for home, and the buses running into town were crowded.

Swaying along with the roll of the bus, he had intended going directly to the church, but when he heard the girl conductor's voice announcing the city hospital, on the spur of the moment he raised his hand to signal that he wished to get off.

The hospital had not been part of his plan. But the girl conductor's call had given him the idea of using his time to make a sick visit to an old foreigner named Durand, whom he had too long neglected.

Durand was an apostate priest. He was a Frenchman who eight years before had been defrocked. He was now deprived of all the blessings and privileges of his priesthood. None of the old Christians ever went near him. Through some covert arrangement made by the Bishop his livelihood was provided

for, but even the Church as far as possible treated the old man
like some contaminated, dangerous monster. About the only
one in the whole diocese to visit Durand occasionally was Father
Sato. Even he went two or three times a year at most. He went
to the hospital only from a sense of obligation in charity, and
from pity.

The pale sunlight of evening was falling on the single-lane
street that ran from the bus stop to the main entrance of the
hospital. A lone woman clutching a medicine bottle was slowly
moving along. She steadied herself by keeping her free hand on
the long grey wall of the hospital. Father Sato was thinking
about the old days as he went past the woman. The old days?
It was only about fifteen years ago, when he had lived with
Durand at the church located in this same end of town called
Sakai-machi. Durand had enjoyed full authority as pastor and
Sato had been the menial curate.

'If it weren't for that fatal assignment to live with him at
Sakai-machi, I wouldn't be saddled with this bothersome duty,
but . . . ,' Father Sato was grumbling to himself, when he was
suddenly conscious of his own selfishness, and he felt ashamed.
He had entertained an unkind thought, a lack of charity
unworthy of a Christian. But never had he felt the least affection
for Durand since the time they lived together. He had no appetite for his duty of going to the hospital several times a year.

The Father Durand whom he knew at the Sakai-machi church
was something of a misfit as a foreign missionary even then.
Apart from being eccentric, Durand had never mixed socially
with his fellow priests among the native clergy. He had a reputation for arrogance.

'I don't know why he ever came to this country.' Father Sato
often heard backbiting remarks like this. The old Christians
at the Sakai-machi church complained endlessly about how he
showed no interest in the Young Men's Club or in the Ladies'
Sodality. Canonically speaking, Durand was the pastor, but he
unloaded the church work onto Sato, his assistant, while he
remained holed up in his room inside the priests' house.

Father Sato often recalled the goings-on at night, and he
wondered. Whenever he woke at night and got up to go to the

toilet, there was always a light burning in Durand's second-storey room, visible from the corridor. If he couldn't do his work decently during the day, what was he engaged on this late at night? Sato looked at the light with a feeling of resentment. The figure of Durand would be sitting stock-still under the dim lamp, both hands supporting his greying temples and his receding hair-line. It was an eerie sight.

Little by little the Christians grew alienated from their pastor. More and more of them went directly to the assistant priest to discuss their spiritual problems, to arrange for a baptism, or to go to confession. No doubt it was hard for the laity to approach Durand's gloomy face, his rather deep-set eyes, his balding forehead. In contrast, their friendly feeling for Sato grew because Sato was jolly in manner and they could understand the speech of a Japanese priest. Father Sato would try to defend Durand by telling the people that they didn't realize all the problems Durand really had.

'Why don't you yourselves try to get a little closer to him?'

But the Christians begged off with the excuse that 'his pronunciation is difficult and we don't understand what he's saying.'

Now that he came to think of it, there was only that one occasion when he had stopped pretending and really let fly at Durand.

'Why don't you be a little more friendly to the parishioners?'

It was at supper one night. The old housekeeper who waited at table had retired to the kitchen. All through the meal Durand had been plying his spoon in silence while he read a foreign theological journal lying open on the table. Sato screwed up his courage and blurted it out. Durand merely raised his deep-set eyes and gave him a blank look.

Father was never clear about just what did occur later on, because it happened only after he was reassigned to become pastor at Kurata-cho. But in due time a nasty rumour of scandal concerning Durand spread through the diocese. The story was that he had established a liaison with some destitute homeless woman whom he had rescued on the night of the big air raid.

At first Father Sato, like all his brother priests, could not believe the story. No matter how eccentric the man might be,

in the last analysis he had trusted Durand just for being a priest.
Nevertheless, Durand himself soon proved the rumour to be a
fact by deserting his post at the church. A scandal like that
shocked the laity, and for the clergy of the diocese it was long
the cause of headaches. It was an embarrassment to the whole
missionary effort.

But with the end of the war people were ready to forget all
sorts of unhappy memories of the past. Thanks to the new
climate of thought it came about that people hardly ever mentioned the Durand scandal. It seemed that the Christians
decided not to reopen old wounds. The diocesan authorities,
without deliberately adopting a policy of merely clamping a lid
on the stinking pot, decided simply to ignore Durand publicly
even while behind the scenes they provided for his support.
They learned to live with the situation. Fortunately for them
Durand developed serious heart trouble, and after he entered
the hospital he rarely set foot outside it. It was a convenient
turn of events.

Father Ginzo Sato felt ashamed by the very existence of
Durand. He himself was one of those priests whose calling and
whose ministry Durand had disgraced. If he did visit the hospital
several times a year, he did it reluctantly and only from a sense
of his obligation as a Christian. To begin with, it wasn't any fun
trying to slip into the hospital without being seen by any of the
Christians.

The entrance area of the hospital was already deserted in the
twilight. Red-thonged slippers for the use of visitors lay scattered about inside the door. The old man in charge of footgear
was seated on the floor above the step with his legs wrapped
around a glazed earthenware *hibachi*. He looked askance at
Father Sato dressed in his long black cassock.

'Visiting hours are over at five o'clock.'

'I'll only be a few minutes.'

The room occupied by Durand was on the second floor, right
at the back. A strong smell of disinfectant suffused the chilly
corridor. A female patient draped in a half-open terrycloth robe
disappeared into the toilet. Now and then a baby started bawling
from somewhere.

When he turned the knob on Durand's door, the greasy body odour peculiar to foreigners hit him right in the nose. One of the walls in the room was strung from end to end with a length of twine on which some large-size union suits were hanging out to dry. Through the evening gloom the familiar pale and puffy face of Durand turned vacuously in the priest's direction.

'It's me,' said Father Sato quietly. 'I haven't been around for a long time, but today I had business out this way, so I took the chance to drop in.'

Father drew from his pocket three packs of Shinsei cigarettes, which he had just bought on the street. He laid them on the bedside table. The old, scruffy table top was whitish with a layer of dust, and was cluttered with dirty dishes and a tea mug full of apple peelings.

'How is your heart since I saw you last?'

'Not good, not bad . . . It's so nice of you, Sato San, to show concern for the likes of me. I'm profoundly grateful.' Durand pressed his hand to the front of his faded dressing gown to emphasize the irony in his words of gratitude. His Japanese was fluent enough, and there was a bite in the way it sounded, enough to nettle Father Sato. Durand as always failed to address his visitor with the proper title of 'Sato Shinpu Sama' (Father) but with the familiar 'Sato San' (Mister), which sounded belittling.

'It has always been his attitude since I lived with him at Sakai-machi. He despises me for not being intellectual enough.' Father Sato gazed a little ruefully at Durand's greying temples and his receding hairline, but he said nothing. Was it because Durand's heart condition was getting progressively worse? At any rate Father Sato thought that his face was even more bloated than when he saw him last.

Suddenly Durand fell into a painful spasm of coughing. He leaned over from the bed to find the range on a small cuspidor where he spat out his slobber in long strings.

'He's a pitiful case. It's come to the point where no one even tries to help him, and so he has turned completely sour. I am the only one that comes to visit him.'

The joyous satisfaction of contemplating his own unselfish

deed began to suffuse the heart of Father Ginzo Sato. He was willing to make allowances. He must tolerate being the target of Durand's sharp tongue, because his antagonist was an old man utterly warped in his whole personality.

'I often thought about coming sooner, but I can never keep ahead of all the parish work. You probably know that for the time being I don't have an assistant pastor.'

'It's because the Church in Japan is so active. You are building new churches one after another, and it's a great strain on manpower. I really mean it.' Durand showed a thin smile as he wiped his mouth with a stained handkerchief. 'But the real question, Sato San, is this, whether the hearts of you Japanese are really good material for Christianity? That's the problem, isn't it?'

'What are you implying, Durand?'

'Will you drink some tea? No fuss, no trouble, I can have it ready in a jiffy. Even in this room of mine there is a simple thing like tea.'

But Durand didn't budge from his sitting position on top of the wrinkled yellowish bedsheets.

'Are you saying that the faith cannot take root in Japan?' Father Sato came right back at Durand in a rather severe tone, wanting to keep him from changing the subject. 'The number of Christians has continued to increase, Durand San, even after you ran out. All the people that belong to my church are fervent Catholics, and the catechumens are all sincere.'

'You think that mere statistical growth is the heart of missionary work.' Durand kept the same faint, derisive smile on his face. 'But I'm a Westerner, and I'm against that way of thinking. How far has Christianity penetrated the hearts of even you Catholics in Japan? I don't trust any of you. There is something in the heart of you Japanese that cannot give itself to this religion. Have you ever thought about that, Sato San?'

Father Sato remained silent. It was not that he was crushed by Durand's sardonic smile or by his frenzied language. Father was thinking that the man must be pitied. Besides having made a disaster of his own life, this foreigner was now speaking blasphemy about the work of evangelization which had once been his own vocation.

'Have you never thought about it, Sato San?' Durand was now in hot pursuit. He rubbed his chin in the palm of his hand. 'Sato San, it isn't just you I'm talking about. Look at the whole Japanese Church, including the foreign priests that come to Japan, because they are all alike. They handle Christian doctrine – how shall I put it? Yes, here's the point – it's because there isn't a single one of them that pays any attention to that enigma in the Japanese heart which makes their work completely sterile.'

'Give me an example, Durand San. What are you talking about?'

'For example . . . ,' Durand grinned again. 'For example, among the Japanese people there seems to be absolutely no concept of sin.'

Father Sato was taken unawares. He kept looking at the sallow, bloated face. He was more than merely jolted, he was stunned. 'The pot is calling the kettle black,' he thought. He was in danger of shouting just such a retort, but kept his mouth shut.

Nevertheless, there crossed his mind in that moment the figure of the nervous student who had approached him for confession after Mass this morning, how from the *prie-dieu* in the quiet secrecy of the confessional the student had blurted out with his putrid breath, 'Even when I had intercourse with my cousin, I didn't have a bad conscience. I never felt dirty. Why not? If I was worried at all, it was only because somebody else might find out what we did.' The words came back to Father Sato.

'Such crazy . . .' This was all he could take. Father Sato rose from his chair, wanting to cut short the blathering of Durand and wanting to exorcize his memory of the student.

Beyond the sickroom window lay the city in the evening dusk. From a distance came the clanging of street cars, the growling of buses. The sea was calm, but it was darkening like the city. Akadaké from beyond the bay had turned to deep purple.

'Well, I won't say any more now about your opinions, Durand

San. But pretty soon we're going to build a little retreat house
at the foot of Akadaké over there. It's all decided. It has been
my dearest hope for a long time. I want to make it a place for
the Christians once or twice a year to escape from the wickedness of the world, close to the peace and quiet of nature, where
they can deepen their faith.'

Father Sato mumbled the words in a mildly sarcastic tone of
voice while he picked up the hat which he had laid on the table
littered with the dirty dishes and the tea mug.

'But that's dangerous, isn't it, Sato San?' exclaimed Durand
with a dash of raillery in his voice. He kept his hands in the
pockets of his threadbare dressing gown. 'How did you hit on
Akadaké for such an important building? A volcano, that's what
Akadaké is. What happens when the volcano blows up?'

'They say that Akadaké won't have another big eruption.
That's what they're saying even at the Observatory. Besides
that, a place for the Christians to lead a holy life will escape
from the evils of nature too.'

'Safe from the evils of society and safe from the evils of
nature?'

'That's what I mean.'

'Well, I'm not so sure.'

The usual thin smile disappeared from Durand's lips. He sat
motionless and looked at the face of Father Sato for some time.

'Durand San, I have to leave,' said Father Sato, pulling on the
door knob. From far down the quiet corridor came the dissonant
tones of an organ. Was one of the nurses playing it? She wasn't
very talented.

'Sato San. Will you take a bet on it? Akadaké is going to
explode. I watch the mountain from this window every day.'
Durand spoke his parting words half in earnest, half in jest.
'Akadaké is absolutely going to explode. Because Evil itself is
a volcano that will never be extinct.'

THREE

The dizziness and the headache which had attacked Suda on the afternoon of the Award Ceremony were completely gone by the next day. In the last few years Suda had usually been waking up in the morning while it was still dark outside. He no longer enjoyed the sensuous comfort of lingering in the quilting as he had enjoyed it before. He was likely to rise early, and the children complained about the noise he made. But on the morning after the Ceremony he slept in soundly, probably because he was physically exhausted from going up on Akadaké.

When a man retires from public service, he begins a different way of life. On that first morning, however, Suda washed his face with the usual feeling of looking ahead to just another day of work at the Observatory. But once he had finished breakfast, and his older boy Ichiro went off to the Company, and his little boy Jiro left for junior high school – ah, the realization came over him that from this day forward there was nothing for him to do. He felt isolated and good for nothing. His daughter-in-law Sakiko and his wife Taka had their own work to do, and they would not be staying close just to keep him company.

The day promised to be terribly long. In the morning he started sorting out a mass of written records covering his active years, which he had piled together in an empty tangerine crate. There were copies of various reports and letters forwarded to the Central Weather Bureau from his distant station in Dairen. He adjusted his reading glasses, spread the papers on his lap, and started browsing through them quietly. The dusty papers recreated those years of living in Dairen, like a dream, when the Empire of Japan still enjoyed its salad days. In Manchuria prices were low, and Suda was young. In order to plot the

course of typhoons he would be taken aboard a plane attached
to the Kanto Army Command and sail through the eye of any
storm that threatened the East China Sea. Of such was the
adventure of living in Dairen.

There were a number of packets wrapped in heavy wax
paper, documents dating from his reassignment to the local
observatory. For the most part they were statistical studies
pertaining to Akadaké, which he had published in the *Meteorological Bulletin*, along with numerous private memoranda on
the same subject. When Suda thought of how probably no one,
not even a university professor in his seismological laboratory,
had ever gathered so great a mass of raw data concerning
that mountain, his heart pounded again with the old feeling of
self-confidence.

Putting together all the correspondence and other items for
which he had no use, he carried them into the garden. He
touched a match to one of the papers, and holding a hand scoop
to control the fire, he lit one from another and watched them
burn. His heart filled with emotion, as anyone's would. His eyes
followed the flakes of white ash flying up on the draughts from
the flame. Each flake of ash bore its own memory from the
second stage of his career. And then he thought of how he
would soon have to get together with Aiba to arrange for the
publication of his *History of the Eruptions of Akadaké*.

The meeting with Aiba occurred one night a full week later.
They sat in a private dining-room at the Eiraku, the Japanese
inn where the City Councilman himself was proprietor. Aiba
seized the initiative and made his proposal first, to the effect
that Suda was to compose a prospectus for the new hotel. He
was to explain the safety of Akadaké and the value of the mountain as a tourist attraction – all this to be one of the documents
for presentation to interested promoters, and for circulation
among the banking interests with whom he hoped to float a
loan.

'At any rate it's going to be more effective if I have a brochure
composed by an expert like you, rather than have an amateur
like me gadding about to explain everything by word of mouth.'

The wide expanse of Aiba's barrel chest showed through the

open hems of his wadded kimono as he grasped a *sake* cup in his big hand and offered it to Suda. Touching the tiny cup to his thin lips, Suda thought that if he was ever going to interject his own proposals, now was the moment to do it.

'So that's it,' said Aiba. 'You want a whole book about Aka-daké.' He leaned over the table to cram his mouth full of meat which he lifted from the pan with his chopsticks, bobbing his head in a token of understanding.

'It's logical all right. If there is going to be a book about that mountain, nobody can match the research you have done.'

'But you see, it's going to be a very technical book, and no commercial publisher will accept it. The book will have to be issued at private expense.'

Aiba's face showed no indications of any real interest. He kept on eating, and he poured another drink. He sensed, however, what Jinpei Suda was going to ask for, and his nimble brain was estimating the degree of self-interest involved in putting this retired public servant under obligation to himself by subsidizing the book.

'Well, I just don't know. I must think about the cost,' said Aiba, and then his foxy eyes lit up for just a moment when he went on to say, 'Let me lay it on the line, Suda San, and you listen to my side.'

There were two parts to his side of the story. First, there was to be in the book a chapter devoted entirely to sightseeing on Akadaké, with emphasis on publicity for the new hotel and a full account of the prodigious achievements of Councilman Aiba in promoting the city's tourist industry. Second, Aiba was to enjoy the exclusive honour of writing a foreword to the book (though Aiba himself used the rather pretentious term 'pre-amble'). These were his two conditions.

'There you have it Suda Kun. You scratch my back and I'll scratch yours.'

Aiba locked his fat arms behind his head and let out a boister-ous laugh. As Jinpei heard the laughing voice, he was well aware that his own labour of half a lifetime would be neatly exploited by this man for his political aggrandizement. He himself had been of a mind to use Aiba, but Aiba was too big for him to control. But at this point there was not a chance of publishing any *History of the Eruptions of Akadaké* except by clinging to this one man. 'It can't be helped,' he said to himself. Suda had always practised the art of getting along in the world by observing the rule, 'If you can't beat them, join them.' He decided to close his eyes to improprieties. He even enhanced his face with a smile when he accepted the man's proposition.

'So let's have another drink, just for a chaser.'

It happened at precisely the moment when he raised his hand to take the *sake* cup offered by Aiba. Jinpei noted some numbness from half-way up his arm down to his fingertips. The *sake* cup fell to the *tatami* floor between his unworkable fingers.

'What's the matter?'

Jinpei's whole frame was trembling with the vertigo and the pain in his head.

'Oh dear, oh dear! Suda San!' Aiba got to his feet with the front hems of his padded kimono still hanging wide open. He clapped his hands together to call the waitress for help.

Jinpei had no recollection of anything after that. When he regained consciousness, he had been carried to his own house and had been put to bed on the floor of the living-room. His mental processes were relatively clear, but his tongue was paralysed and he couldn't utter a word.

Under a dim bulb hanging from the ceiling, Taka and his oldest son Ichiro were squatting near the bed, talking together in hushed tones. Suda heard their voices indistinctly as though he were watching them from a distance.

'This is really a mess,' said Ichiro, apparently thinking that Suda was still unconscious. 'Low blood pressure is not a thing that's going to correct itself in a month or two. The hospital is going to cost a lot of money, and it isn't fair to saddle me with the whole responsibility. And, Mother, I don't want to catch you pushing off on Sakiko the dirty job of cleaning up his toilet messes.'

Taka started to give her son a piece of her own mind but Ichiro was not about to be shushed, and he came right back at her.

'Mother, I'll grant that the old man always made you wait on

him hand and foot while he just took it for granted. But that's
beside the point.'

Suda didn't understand the argument. He made an effort to
move his paralysed tongue, and then slipped back into his coma.

FOUR

It was raining, and the rain had been falling incessantly since the night before. One by one the drops of rain were slowly running down the window pane.

Durand was sitting close to the window in his battered rattan chair. From time to time he pulled a snotty mouse-coloured handkerchief from the pocket of the dressing gown tucked around his puffy body. He blew his nose fortissimo. Then he wiped away the tear drops running from his eyes. For the last six months a chronic discharge from his nose and eyes had blotched his face. Nobody knew what caused the excessive drip.

'*Sacré vieux chien*! You poor old son of a bitch . . . ,' he reviled himself, silently forming the words with his lips. '*Sacré vieux chien . . .*'

The city he could see below him lay soggy with the dull and gloomy rain. In good weather the clatter of cars and buses, a whistle from the excursion boat out on the bay, the banging noises of the factories, all the varied, nerve-racking sounds of city life carried into his room along with the dust that rode the breezes. On a rainy day like this, however, the city was eerily quiet. The warren of houseroofs made an abstract pattern limned in graphite. There were ugly stains and streaks on the concrete walls of apartment houses. Cars moved slowly along the leaden pavements. The city was ashen grey. Akadaké lay under a cover of cloud with only the deep-black foot of the mountain protruding.

'It was raining that day too . . . wasn't it? Come to think of it, it was snowing.' Once again the paranoid Durand was beginning to finger his old wounds. Every time he did it, he would realize afterwards that it wasn't any help at all to pick the scars open, but he didn't really have anything else to occupy his mind. 'When Father Sato came in yesterday,' mused Durand, 'he was probably thinking about how I left the Church, how it was just eight years ago that I was unfrocked. But not only Father Sato. The ordinary people are no doubt recalling it too, thinking about what happened that night of the air raid on the city. The only thing they were indignant about is that I gave shelter in the church to that utterly destitute woman. But a sin, if what happened really was a sin . . . It's like a poisonous weed. When you dig it out, you find that the weed had ramifying roots reaching deep into the ground. When I was excommunicated eight years ago, I was still the man that I had been before, product of the roots I always had.'

'The main root reaches back to . . .' A child was laid face up on an iron bedstead whose white paint was peeling off in parts. A white gauze covered the child's face. The child's mother and his grandmother cowered silently in the narrow space between the bed and the wall. The glow from a candle in Durand's right hand threw their elongated shadows on the wall. When Durand took the corner of the white cloth with his left hand and lifted it, the signs of an agonizing death were still visible on the boy's brow. His eyes and mouth were pinched shut, and the whole face seemed uncommonly strained in the chiaroscuro gleam from the candle.

'Shall I get Dr Sasaki to fill out the death certificate?'

A young nurse opened the door and raised her voice. Did she only then sense the mood within the room? At any rate she slipped quietly back into the corridor. All of this was twenty-two years ago, and only the second year after Durand had assumed his post at the church in Sakai-machi.

If Durand had not fallen sick with croupous pneumonia in the winter of that year, he would never have had occasion to exert himself on behalf of this lad or his mother and grandmother. Going back in memory he recalled that it all began after Mass on a morning near the end of January. He had felt a severe headache while offering Mass. When he read the Gospel, the letters of the Latin text appeared to be swimming about behind a sheet of isinglass. Every time he went down in genuflection he felt his whole weight being sucked right into the ground. Making it back to the sacristy after Mass, he promptly collapsed with a great clatter of the sacred vessels. Three or four men came running in, startled at the noise, and they carried him in their own hands to the nearby Wakita Hospital.

The fever of the pneumonia continued for several days with his temperature running between 103 and 106 degrees. His lips and nostrils broke out in tetters. At intervals in his delirium he rolled up the whites of his eyes and was dimly aware of the rimless glasses and the medical garb of a lady doctor leaning over him. He was vaguely conscious of her plunging a needle into his arm. The tense face and sweaty forehead of the lady doctor went in and out of focus.

On the morning of the third day the fever suddenly vanished. The terrible headache which had so tortured him until the night before was simply wiped away. Even outside, it was the first nice day after a long spell of bad weather. When a nurse's aide offered him a glass of tangerine juice, he thought it tasted delicious.

The aide told him, 'You were able to recover fast because Dr Tsugawa went all out in taking care of you.'

'Which one is Dr Tsugawa?' asked Durand.

'You foreigner, you! What an ingrate.' The nurse's aide laughed in amusement, exposing her dark red gums. 'It's the lady doctor who's been treating you all along.'

That morning Durand expressed his gratitude to the lady doctor named Tsugawa when she came to him on her regular morning rounds. He was sitting awkwardly on the bed, his hairy shins protruding from the bath kimono which he had received as a gift some time ago from one of the parishioners.

The lady doctor was short in stature, and with her rimless glasses she gave an impression of being somewhat timorous.

'Our foreign patient is really healthy!' The nurse's aide triumphantly introduced Durand to the doctor. She was, in contrast to the doctor, a little overly familiar with Durand.

'Your line of work and mine have much in common, don't you

think? We are both devoted to curing human beings.' Dr Tsugawa spoke as she pressed her fingers to his bare-skinned,
hairy chest.

To cover his embarrassment Durand assumed his role of
missionary priest. 'Back in Europe there are many people of
strong Christian faith working in the medical profession,
but . . .'

While she applied the stethoscope, Durand noted the cheap
stockings which had crumpled into transverse wrinkles, the
badly run-down heels of her unpolished shoes. As she was
preparing the ampule for an injection, the doctor's face seemed
old beyond her years. She was a woman prematurely faded with
the cares of life.

'I have one little boy,' she remarked softly, winding up the
tubes of the stethoscope. Her eyes blinked rapidly behind the
rimless spectacles. 'For a long time I've been thinking of sending
him to one of the mission schools.'

'If that's the case, why not bring the boy along and come to
see me at the church?'

When the doctor left the room, accompanied by the nurse
who was hugging the charts, the aide again displayed her dark
red gums and began her usual chatter. Durand understood that
the lady doctor was a widow; that she had lost her husband,
who was an engineer, three years ago, that she was left with
an only child, a sickly little fellow. Nevertheless, four or five
days later, when he returned to the church fully recovered,
Durand completely forgot the lady doctor.

In that period of his life he was a fairly busy man. Besides
the various duties directly connected with being pastor at the
Sakai-machi church, he went outside the city once a week to
the convent of the Bernadette Sisters. There he regularly
heards the nuns' confessions, and from time to time he became
involved as a consultant to the religious community on matters
of policy. The Sisters had a building near their convent called
Magdela House, a place for the rehabilitation of what are
referred to as women of the streets. The Prefectural government had frequently endorsed the institution, and even the
newspaper had run pictures of the girls pumping away at their

sewing machines and sitting through their English language classes.

While Durand sat there in his creaky rattan chair close to the rainy window, thinking back about the lady doctor named Tsugawa, another quite different situation came painfully to mind. It had begun one evening late in autumn. Durand was riding in company with one of the nuns on the rickety bus heading towards the city. The nun was Sister Makino. There were no other passengers on the bus, and the two sat in silence near the back. Durand was returning to the church, but Sister Makino was on her way into the city to fetch back to Magdela House a girl by the name of Hanaë Toda, who had run away that morning.

Behind the barren trees lining the roadside could be seen the black soil of extensive fields of vegetables. The bus went bouncing along the country roads that ran between the cultivated fields.

'This is the third case we have had. Why do these children want to go back to the quagmire, back to that wretched way of life? I can't understand it.' Sister Makino muttered the words through a handkerchief held to her face, and the words conveyed a touch of anger. She used the term 'children', but the nun herself was hardly more than twenty-five or twenty-six years old. To be honest, the case of Hanaë was by no means unique, because every month or so there was a runaway from Magdela House. Some of the girls could not stand the strictly disciplined and sheltered way of life provided by the Sisters. They went back to the streets to sell their bodies again.

'What is the word for it in Japanese?' Durand was fumbling for the equivalent of 'gigolo', as he strained to find the words to ask if Hanaë by any chance did not belong to some pimp.

The nun blushed at the word 'pimp' but she said, 'Yes, she does. And yet in the diary that we make the girls keep, she wrote that she was mistreated by the man, that he sometimes beat her up and kicked her. I can't believe that she would go back for more of that.'

Durand recalled meeting Miss Hanaë Toda only once. It was

on the occasion of his regular visit to the convent, just two weeks before. The inmates were playing dodge ball in the inner courtyard, under the Sisters' supervision as usual. There was one girl with a soiled bandage wrapped around her head. She held both hands inside her sleeves as though she was cold, sitting there on the stone steps in the pale autumn sunlight. It was Hanaë. One of the Sisters explained to Durand that the girl was forbidden to take any exercise because her lungs were weak.

When they pulled up at the stop in front of Police Headquarters, Sister Makino got off the bus, trailing behind her the fluttering hems of her black veil. The friendly Chief of Police was always ready to be of assistance to Magdela House in cases of this kind.

The next day Durand got a telephone call. It was Sister Makino, and the message was clear. Miss Hanaë Toda had indeed gone back to her man. But worse than that, Sister went on to say, the girl was running a fever, and she was bedded down in a second-storey room above a disreputable back street bistro run by the pimp's older sister. The nun could not return the girl to Magdela House in her sick condition. In this emergency she wanted to find a decent hospital willing to admit Hanaë.

'Father, what about the hospital where you were treated that time?"

'I know what you mean.' Durand recalled the middle-aged lady doctor in the cheap hoisery with the transverse wrinkles, the low-top shoes with the run-down heels. 'I'll telephone there and see what can be done.'

'This girl is going to be the death of me.' The nun's voice sounded utterly worn out on the other end of the line. 'She is a completely different person from what she was at our place. Father . . .'

'Yes, what is it?'

'She keeps crying that it's better to die close to her man, no matter how he abuses her. It's come to the point where I can't understand the reasoning of these girls.'

*   *   *

Fresh drops of rain again went running slowly down the window.
The hospital was quiet in the hush of approaching evening.
Every now and then from far down the corridor he heard the
squeal of the toilet door when somebody opened it, probably
one of the patients. Durand didn't know whether Sister Makino
was still at Magdela House or not. He blew his nose again in the
dirty handkerchief and rubbed his eyes. Even now, twenty-two
years after the event, Sister Makino probably still didn't understand Hanaë's motive for running away. The nuns could not
conceive of how a woman could forsake the clean sheets and
the nourishing food of a religious house and prefer to gasp away
her life at the side of a man who kicked her around and beat
her. Not only the nuns, but from Durand's knowledge of them,
none of the Japanese Christians could have any sympathy for a
girl like that. He realized that back then at that time in his own
life, he had shared their attitude. With one hand he pulled the
ravelled blanket from the bed and wrapped it around his legs,
because the room was getting chilly as the night came on.

'I was acting from an attitude of smugness, like theirs, when
I tried to convert that widowed lady doctor.'

It was a rainy Sunday afternoon not long before Easter when
Dr Tsugawa unexpectedly appeared at the church with her little
boy. Even while he was in the hospital, Durand never thought
that Dr Tsugawa really had the presence of a lady physician.
Today she wasn't even dressed in her hospital whites, and the
skirts of her raincoat were splattered with mud. More than ever
she looked the part of a little Japanese housewife wizened with
domestic cares, and her peeked boy in spectacles stood beside
her dressed in a school uniform.

'It was a big imposition on you the other day, with no more
warning than a telephone call.' As Durand expressed his thanks
over the recent emergency, he stole a glance at the child,
who was gawking stupidly without the least hint of any bow in
salutation. 'Is this your little boy?' he said.

When they moved into the rectory parlour, with its odour of
varnish, Dr Tsugawa looked at her son and remarked, 'He's a
sickly lad, and I kept him out of school for a whole year.'

She went on to explain that the boy's name was Nobuo, and

that she would like to have him withdrawn from his present school and admitted to Eiko Academy, a Catholic mission school.

'Since he's an only child, he has been pampered to some extent, but Eiko enjoys an excellent reputation, and I think he will get a solid training there.'

The lady doctor's delicate voice mumbled on that it was quite presumptuous on her part to come for such a discussion, but that she didn't know anyone else connected with the Christian religion. Durand assured her that he would take the matter up with the Father Principal at the school, although he wasn't sure what could be done.

As he saw the two of them to the door, Durand laid his big hand on the boy's head. The boy flinched at his touch and pulled away, but his ill-natured face stayed furtively fixed on the priest. 'A repulsive kid,' thought Durand.

It was drizzling outside. Durand slipped his stockinged feet into a pair of sandals and went with them as far as the gate.

'When did your husband pass away?' he asked.

'Three years ago, when we lived in Yahata,' said the doctor with a touch of wistful loneliness. She stood there in her *geta* designed with toe-guards to protect against the rain. 'My husband was an engineer by profession, but a child without a father lacks the discipline for anything like that.'

'With my father it was just the opposite. My father was a martinet, but children need strict training,' agreed Durand.

Without so much as a bow of good-bye Nobuo started off by himself, jumping from one mud puddle to the next in his high boots. Durand was convinced that the boy was an undisciplined brat. Nevertheless, a week later he met with Father Rietsch at Eiko Academy out near Shirayama Park. Father Rietsch was a bull-headed priest from Alsace. He shook his head in refusal. Then he was surprised at the other's persistence, Durand going so far as to say that he himself would assume full responsibility.

'The lad's a Christian, is he?'

'Not yet, but I want to try to make him one,' Durand answered with honesty. So it came about that Nobuo was permitted to transfer.

'At that time my intention was only to help the mother and her child.' Durand sat blinking his eyes, still brooding over the old days. 'But how difficult it is for a man in his conscience to discern true benevolence from his lust for controlling the lives of others.'

Certainly from that day forward Durand made every effort to enrich the lives of Dr Tsugawa and her dependents. Say what he would, that he was forcing his own ideas on the mother and her son, it certainly was never done from any conscious bad will. The doctor's home was in Izumi-machi, not too far away. There were three identical bungalows, built around a little garden, and the Tsugawa home was the house on the right as he faced the garden from the street. Sliding open the front door, he saw Nobuo's shoes and *geta* scattered about in the entrance way. The interior of the house was a trifle untidy wherever he looked. The smell from the inside privy vaguely permeated the place. Then on those nights when the doctor was detained at the hospital, little Nobuo and his grandmother, who wore a white sweat band attached to the collar of her kimono, had to wait forever for their supper.

Durand remembered nights like that. Every week on Tuesday and Friday he went there to explain the catechism for the doctor and her old mother-in-law. Whenever the old lady, exhausted from the long day, began to slide her head in a doze, Dr Tsugawa would glance at Durand nervously.

Two months later Durand received a letter from Father Rietsch at Eiko Academy. It carried all sorts of complaints about Nobuo – he lacks discipline; his grades are poor; he tells lies. After detailing the charges, Father Rietsch exhorted Durand to stricter supervision of the boy.

Next day Durand met with the doctor.

'It's not good for a child to be living with his grandmother. You ought to make the boy live in the dormitory on campus.' Durand spoke sharply to the doctor, while she sat there meekly inspecting her hands which were resting on her lap. 'If I were you, that's what I would do. What Nobuo needs most is strict discipline in his upbringing.'

From the shadows of the room the subject of their

conversation, the boy Nobuo, kept looking covertly at him with the snaky eyes that always nettled Durand.

'Nobuchan, what would you yourself like to do?' the worried mother asked her son.

That sufficed to ignite Durand. He laid the blame on her, and he roared, 'Japanese mothers coddle their children. In my country we beat them with a whip until they are fifteen years old.'

To tell the truth, Durand simply didn't like this whey-faced Nobuo with the dismal glint in his eye. He didn't like the boy, and yet again it was not from any malicious intent that he separated the boy from his mother, even though they had been living peaceably together since the father died. As a matter of fact, Durand was a rather busy man, but he spent all the leisure he could find in caring for the needs of this family. For example, on Sundays when Dr Tsugawa was away from home with her duties at the hospital, Durand took thought for the loneliness of Nobuo, who was away from the dormitory for the weekend. There was even one occasion when he brought the boy to the church to spend the day. Durand had no experience in handling children of his own, and to make matters worse, this child was a Japanese. He didn't know how to entertain a child. He took the boy into his own room and sat down with him to read aloud from a Life of Christ done in an easy-to-read translation. But Nobuo, who happened to be wearing a dirty bandage on his neck, just sat there with empty eyes gazing out of the window to infinity.

'I suppose you would rather read by yourself. How would that be?'

Durand was depressed to think that reading a Japanese book in his harsh foreign accent could never hold the child's interest. So he placed the book on the boy's lap, along with an apple, and quietly slipped from the room. He spent almost an hour walking up and down in the churchyard, reading the Divine Office from his breviary. When he came back to the room the boy was standing with his face at the window and hands in his pockets.

He was watching a pair of sparrows perched in the leafless branches of a tree.

No matter what he tried, Durand could never get the boy to show in his face the slightest sign of interest. No wonder that sometimes he actually began to hate the boy. Yet he blamed only himself for the feeling of hate, and once in his desperation he tried another expedient, inviting Nobuo out for a walk. He was utterly insensitive to the embarrassment that Nobuo felt when seen walking with a foreigner.

Along the street Nobuo constantly lagged behind, keeping his distance as much as possible. Once he was looking at a picture that he had pulled from his pocket when Durand suddenly turned around and spotted him. Durand's suspicion was aroused when Nobuo made a hasty move to hide the picture he was holding.

'Nobuo, let me see it, that picture!'

Having forcibly seized the abomination, he saw that it was a cinema handbill. Some starlet in a bikini was striking a sexy pose, standing on top of a rock, her right hand resting on her head. Durand's features tensed with a terrible anger. He tore the handbill in two. Then he slapped Nobuo's face with his open palm.

He advised Nobuo that the only reason he had taken pains to have him admitted to the dormitory was his hope that the discipline there would cure the boy of his shiftless ways and his habit of telling lies.

Knocked out of bed at six in the morning, the boys went to Mass in a body, Catholics or not. Then came breakfast, then classes. When school was over and supper finished, they assembled again for night prayers and examination of conscience. This was the routine modelled on monastic life that Durand had followed as a boy in the minor seminary at Grenoble, and he was convinced that a rigidly structured daily routine was good for a boy like Nobuo.

But within the month this high expectation too was betrayed by the timid voice of the lady doctor coming to see him at the church.

'The boy keeps saying that he wants to come home,' pleaded the mother as she watched for the reaction on Durand's face.

'At first I scolded him for that kind of talk, but after all, he really is a child of delicate constitution, you know.'

'What are you going to do? Send him back to that other school?' Durand shook his head in disapproval. 'I promised Father Rietsch, the Principal, that I would assume responsibility. Don't you realize that it is your duty as well as mine to develop that boy into a real man?'

Some time in the winter of that year Nobuo was brought home, not because Durand had relented, but because the dormitory prefect himself was worried about the pupil's health. The prefect reported that the boy's appetite had noticeably fallen off, that he wasn't eating and was losing weight. This time, of course, Durand could make none of his harsh comments. At home the boy stayed in bed all day in the absence of his mother. His face was slightly flushed and feverish. Just to be on the safe side, they took X-rays at the hospital, only to discover a lesion had developed in the left lung behind the clavicle bone of his puny chest.

On hearing the news Durand immediately ran to the hospital and met Dr Tsugawa in the night-duty room, where the light falling from a low-powered bulb was enough to reveal on the doctor's face the deep shadows of worry and fatigue around her eyes.

'What do you think we should do? A lesion like that is hard to treat.'

Durand said, 'Pray.'

'If I were to receive baptism . . . ,' said the mother in a kind of pitiable prayer, holding both hands to the sides of her head. 'And if the boy recovers . . .'

Durand experienced a feeling of deep sympathy for this exhausted woman. Joy welled up in his heart at the thought that all the pains he had gone to for a whole year had not been in vain.

'If it is for your own spiritual welfare, God will certainly deign to cure little Nobuo.'

One month later, on the Feast of St Mathias, Doctor Tsugawa and her mother-in-law were baptized at the church in Sakai-machi.

But Nobuo showed no speedy signs of improvement. Durand found time again on Sunday afternoon to visit the hospital. The boy had slid his somewhat feverish face down off the pillow and was gazing out of the window.

'Remember that God is going to help you get well.' Durand spoke gentle words of encouragement with an unaccustomed tremor in his voice. This time there was not a wisp of that animosity towards the child which he had always felt before. 'When you get strong again, you can receive baptism too, just like your good mother.'

Durand failed to notice the faint glint of hostility that passed across the boy's eyes. He knelt right there by the bed, and he prayed from his heart for the life of Nobuo.

The muffled sound of voices engaged in conversation came through the wall from the next room, which had been unoccupied until this morning. Durand had been sitting with his eyes closed. He opened his eyes and cocked his ears to catch the words, but he could not hear what the voices were saying.

The rain still fell relentlessly. The dark of night pervaded the room, and it was cold. He had his feet wrapped in the blanket, but his legs ached with cold down to the tips of his toes. There was a sturdy cherry wood cane leaning against the wall. It served Durand for a gentleman's walking stick as he leaned on it and moved into the corridor. He had bought the cane a long time ago at Shirahama, on the day of an outing to Akadaké with the young men of his parish.

Coming back from the toilet, he passed in front of the room next to his own. The door was half open.

'We will let him stay in this private ward temporarily, and then we can move him to one of the big wards. Will that be satisfactory?'

'Yes, please do it that way.'

Durand overheard the voice of a little old woman speaking with one of the doctors. A small name card was pinned to the door, and the still wet brush-strokes showed the Chinese characters for 'Jinpei Suda'.

There was more time to kill before supper would be served,

so Durand sat down once more in the wicker chair that threatened to fall apart.

'At that time everything I tried to do turned out the same way. And the cause was always the same.' When Durand woke up to his illusions, it was always too late to prevent the damage.

In the month of March, he recalled, in a year when the snowfall was below normal, Nobuo died at an hour approaching dawn, on a night memorable for the long delayed snow that covered the city in white. The boy was laid face up on the paint-chipped bedstead, his face covered with a white gauze. Dr Tsugawa and her old mother-in-law were huddled together silently in the space between the bed and the wall. The candle held by Durand threw their elongated shadows on the wall. With a trembling hand he took a corner of the white cloth and lifted it. Traces of the death agony were still faintly visible on the boy's brow.

'Eternal rest grant unto him, O Lord, and let perpetual light . . . ,' intoned Durand from the bedside, but he was interrupted by the young nurse opening the door and calling, 'Shall I get Dr Sasaki to fill out the death certificate?' Then she beat a hasty retreat.

'Eternal rest grant unto him, O Lord . . .' When Durand again started to recite the official Prayers for the Dead, he was interrupted this time by the quiet voice of the old woman crouched on the other side of the bed. 'Listen to me,' she said to the lady doctor. 'Whatever we do, we have to bury Nobuo in the Buddhist way. Because the boy's father was a Buddhist.'

Durand cut her short, but she only narrowed the slits of her eyes and shook her head in stubborn opposition.

'You can't do it. Because the boy never liked you. In fact he hated you.'

Durand walked back alone to the church. It was still snowing, and he turned up the collar of his overcoat. At first it was like a terrible fire raging in his belly, the flames fed by resentment and humiliation. 'I did everything that I'm supposed to do. I did absolutely everything that I'm supposed to do, and yet . . .'

There was not a shadow of human life on the pre-dawn streets, white in the powdery snow whirling down, swirling up. He turned a corner and a powerful blast of wind hit him in the face. Durand dug his stiffened fingers deep into his pockets. He took hold of the little crucifix attached to the end of his rosary beads.

Arriving at the church, he fumbled with the bunch of keys hanging from his belt and opened the heavy wooden door to the chapel. He knelt down on a *prie-dieux* and stayed there for a long time in the dark. He tried to pray for Nobuo and his mother, but deep in his subconscious very different sentiments were churning; little by little they welled up to consciousness and overpowered him. Only a short while before, as he was running down the steps towards the hospital exit, he heard the noisy footsteps of somebody pursuing him. It was Dr Tsugawa. She held on to the railing. Her face was hideously distorted, splotched with sweat and tears. She cried out to him, 'Father. I am all alone. What shall I do? What can I do now?'

He had no answer.

'Because I did everything I was supposed to do . . .' He tried to reassure himself. But he knew that he was lying. He felt that his soul was frozen stiff. He joined his hands in prayer to God, to Whom he had prayed throughout his life. God did not answer.

'*Sacré vieux chien*, you poor old son of a bitch . . . ,' muttered Durand in self-derision while he wiped his dripping nose again, then daubed his eyes with the handkerchief. '*Sacré vieux chien, sacré vieux chien.*'

And so another day turned into night. The long waking hours spent in turning over old memories came again to an end. But all the events he had recalled today were nothing more than a specimen drawn from his career. Tomorrow he would recall a different chain of bitter memories. He would spend another day sipping at the vile broth. Saving souls, making converts – if priestly work had been for him the simple task it was for that Japanese priest named Sato, then perhaps he himself would have survived without being excommunicated from the Church. But in his own case, whatever he tried in wanting to do God's work had ended up ironically in disaster, in tragic consequences. Moreover, God was always silent. God did not answer his prayers. God was only trifling with Durand, as though he were nothing but a kind of gewgaw.

Pulling the blanket off his legs, Durand put his face to the window. He pressed his forehead against the glass, saying it over and over to himself. *'Sacré vieux chien . . . sacré vieux chien.'*

The evening mist and the rain had painted out the city with heavy grey. The sea was painted black. Akadaké lay submerged in the low cloud cover. Durand gazed at the broadspreading foot of the mountain. He recalled the retreat house that Father Sato talked of building – amid the beauties of nature, withdrawn from the evils of the world, a house to deepen one's faith. If sin were a thing to be so easily avoided, then perhaps he himself would have finished without becoming the decrepit old son of a bitch that he was.

'Go ahead and explode! Go ahead and explode!' Durand was actually hoping that some day without warning the mountain would vomit its fire and smoke, retch with its lava, destroy everything – as he had destroyed it all with his own life.

FIVE

Less than a month after Jinpei Suda was admitted to the hospital, Akadaké suddenly erupted.

The forenoon of the day was much like any other. The sky was partly cloudy, and there was a little nip in the air for the people of this provincial city in southern Japan, but even so, the weather was notably warmer than in Tokyo and the other great centres of population. With the approach of Christmas and the end of another year, the main business district, called Hatayacho, was alive with people moving up and down the main street in greater numbers than in any other season. The only large department store was the Mitsukoshi, where from the midmorning opening of doors a vast throng of housewives were out to take advantage of the special Winter Sale. They were picking over the merchandise, looking for bargains in household needs and shopping for the traditional exchange of gifts at the year's end. Along the street some of the shops were anticipating the season by trimming their fronts with clusters of bamboo and pine sprigs to greet the New Year.

Even so, just a step away from the commercial atmosphere of the main thoroughfare lay a quiet residential neighbourhood where before the big air raid there had stood intact the ancient Buddhist temples and the mansions of the old Samurai class. Around noon a lame old man, the umbrella mender, was winding his way from one narrow street to another. He could hear a popular song from the radio playing in a house somewhere.

Again in contrast to Tokyo, the city was small enough to allow many working people to grab a bite to eat at home instead of packing a box lunch to eat at their place of employment.

Before the siren wailed in broad daylight no one in his wildest dreams imagined that Akadaké was about to explode.

It came at high noon, when the people were at lunch. At first they seemed to hear a dull rumble as of distant thunder. Then a sudden ear-splitting detonation. Houses shook, windows rattled. People panicked and ran into the streets, where they beheld a black column of smoke rising into the sky beyond the bay. The top of the column expanded into a shape like the round head on a sprig of cauliflower. They watched the head uncoil.

'It's like the cloud of the atom bomb,' they said.

A two-kilometre stretch of open water lies between Akadaké and the city. When they saw that the smoke was rising straight up, the people sensed that there was no immediate danger. They went back to stuffing their mouths with gobs of rice and watched the display while munching their food.

The uproar from Akadaké was the talk of the town all afternoon. Employees neglected their work and gathered by the windows to watch any movement in the cloud of smoke that continued to top the volcano. The radio newscast at three o'clock featured public service announcements to further reassure the citizens. The announcer stressed that there was no cause for alarm in spite of the fact that today's eruption was totally unexpected even at the Weather Bureau. He went on to explain that in the past two weeks the seismograph had recorded no tremors of any kind that might have portended volcanic activity. Investigations now in progress showed that today's event did not involve any release of the dangerous magma. The phenomenon was described as merely the sudden discharge of gases trapped at the crater mouth. There was not a single fatality or casualty of any kind, even among the sightseers hiking on the mountain. A trace of volcanic ash had fallen on the hamlets of Ichifusa and Furusato towards the south end of the island, but thankfully it was not enough to injure man or beast, or even to affect adversely the land under cultivation.

Be that as it may, for several days running the newspaper and the radio faithfully reported on the movements of Akadaké. Yet even before a week had passed, it seemed that people had completely forgotten the event. Akadaké itself went back to relinquishing from its peak the usual plume of thin smoke rising peacefully into the sky, as if that sudden explosion had never occurred. At the Mitsukoshi Department Store in Hataya-cho the banner announcing the Winter Sale gave way to a huge facsimile of Santa Claus suspended on the building's façade to herald the current Christmas Sale. On the side streets of the business district some of the smaller shops already featured the traditional herring roe and slabs of salted salmon wrapped with straw matting. The lame old umbrella mender was still on his slow-moving rounds through the residential lanes, where all he could hear was the quiet sound of another piece of popular music on the radio in somebody's house. Everything was normal. Nothing had changed.

Jinpei Suda heard the explosion of Akadaké from his bed in the hospital. When the cannon blast rattled the windows in the ward, he opened his eyes and without a word cocked his ears to catch the reverberations. But his wife Taka was startled to her feet. Then Suda strained to ask with his tongue-tied mouth, 'Where? . . . Where?'

Taka moved to the window. She told him that the emission was not from the side of the mountain but apparently from the very top. Suda relaxed, buried his unshaven chin in the pillow, and closed his eyes again.

Even though Suda had not seen the smoke with his own eyes, he knew that the eruption was only a momentary thing. Tomorrow Akadaké would be the same old decrepit mountain. If today's emission came from the top, he could even predict how high the smoke would rise.

Just as he had surmised, on the following day he saw from the hospital window that Akadaké had resumed its old forlorn appearance. Suda was moved by the ominous feeling that he and the mountain were treading the same mysteriously fateful course. Just when his own body was stricken, Akadaké reacted to his condition with its own lugubrious blast. And then Akadaké returned in sympathy to the silence that matched so well the languid days of Jinpei's rest in bed. Both he and the mountain were moving towards death. On and off this thought would ramble through his mind. He lay there gazing at the sunlight flickers on the ceiling.

That evening, as his wife held the bedpan to him and waited for him to release his water, Suda asked her, 'On the night of my stroke, Ichiro was there talking at the bedside, wasn't he?'

'What are you trying to say?'

Suda thought better of it, and went silent.

He didn't know why on this particular evening, a month after the event, he had suddenly recalled that particular scene. But there it was.

He had been eating dinner with City Councilman Aiba at the Eiraku Inn when he was stricken, and he regained consciousness back in the living-room of his own house. From the time he took sick until just a few days ago his mind was so confused and vague that the effort of trying to recall the sequence of events was more than he could manage. Yet bits and pieces had remained with him, details of the living-room scene, the faded spots on the ceiling, and the Shinto talisman pinned to the wall post to protect from the danger of fire. Ichiro and Taka were sitting on the floor next to his bedding. They were speaking in hushed voices. Suda heard the voices fuzzily, like voices coming from afar.

'We're in a fix, aren't we?' This was the voice of Ichiro. 'There will be the hospital expenses, and it isn't right to saddle me with the whole responsibility. And I warn you, Mother, don't leave the old man's toilet needs and that sort of thing entirely up to Sakiko.'

Then Taka took to berating Ichiro, calling him dirty names.

'Mother, I know that you have been nursing a grudge against the old man for a long, long time. And he's never paid the least attention to what you felt.'

'What are you talking about?'

'Well, let's forget it. But I know what's been going on.'

Jinpei had no recollection of anything after that. He had lapsed back into a coma.

Nevertheless, at the present moment, along with those eerie impressions of the dark living-room, the talisman fixed to the wall and the other details, the talk between Ichiro and Taka came back to him.

'Have you finished passing your water?'

'Yeh.'

Taka wrapped the bottle of urine in a sheet of newspaper and left the room to wash it out in the toilet. Jinpei heard in a haze the sound of her slippers fading down the corridor, then in the distance a squeal from the swinging toilet door. Jinpei wondered whether it was true that Taka resented him. When he was young, at least after the two of them were married, Jinpei had never laid a hand on any other woman. It was not that he treasured his wife for being the only woman in the world. It was rather that his faint-hearted character always disposed him to think first about social appearances. He had lived as man and wife with Taka for thirty-two years, and Jinpei could not but admit that there had been times when he acted the rather tyrannical master at home. But that was true of any husband from his own generation, and Taka had no reason to complain.

When Taka came back from the toilet, she noticed her husband studying her intently. She spoke in a low voice, as though confiding to him alone some secret affair of unimaginable importance.

'Down in the toilet I happened to meet with that foreigner gentleman from the room next door. I was really startled. His name is Durand, or something like that.'

'Oh?' said Jinpei.

But after that simple reaction, he kept his mouth shut. Like a child he felt put to shame at the way in which Taka had interrupted him with the solemn revelation of the toilet encounter.

Sometime in the morning on a day in the week following the mountain eruption, they heard the boisterous voice of City Councilman Aiba coming from the corridor.

'Nurse! I say there. Suda Kun's room is down this way, isn't it? I've been here before, but I'm not familiar with the lay-out. I'm a little confused.'

Then with the slapping noise from his loose-fitting slippers Aiba came on to open the door of Suda's room. He wore a

fur-trimmed Inverness cape across his shoulders. He seized a
basket of fruit from the hands of a man behind him, who seemed
to be a taxi driver.

'My apologies. I'm always thinking about coming to see you
again, but you know I've been so busy.'

He laid the basket of fruit on the edge of the bed, and said
to Taka, who was nervously trying to straighten the sheets,
'Mrs Suda, don't make a fuss over this thing. It's nothing at all.'

As usual, it was quite apparent that he had been drinking. His
fat neck was flushed red as it protruded from his Satsuma-style,
splashed-pattern kimono.

'Well, you look much better than I had expected.'

This was Aiba's second visit, but nevertheless he went on to
relate again in great detail the scene of Jinpei's collapse at the
Eiraku Inn, all for the repeated benefit of Suda and Taka. At
any rate, he said, he himself was always worried about his own
blood pressure problem, but even so, when Suda Kun toppled
over, he did not permit the chambermaids to move him. He
bragged over and over again how that was the most intelligent
thing to do. Then after discussing the patient's present condition, Aiba suddenly became serious.

'Not to change the subject, Suda San. But the reason I came
over today was to get your advice on another question. Akadaké
exploded recently, and after that I got wind of a strange report
just the other day.'

To explain the strange report, Aiba drew from the bosom of
his kimono something wrapped in a kerchief. He opened the
kerchief and unfolded in front of Suda a single copy of a thin
magazine.

'Here it is, on this page here.'

The magazine was a learned journal of a type that no one
could expect to find in the hands of an ignoramus like Aiba. In
the journal a certain Tokyo University professor by the name
of Maejima had written a new theory on Akadaké. Aiba began
to explain that he couldn't even read the thing, but he had made
his son read it and tell him what it was about.

According to the local weather station, the recent eruption
of Akadaké involved no emission of the dangerous magma, but

was limited to a release of gas trapped near the crater mouth, and consequently the explosion was only a passing phenomenon. But Dr Maejima's opinion directly contradicted the conclusion drawn at the Observatory. Dr Maejima was a young scholar who had devoted himself to volcanic gas for the last ten years. He had fixed his attention on the discovery that whenever a volcano erupted, the gas emission included enormous amounts of the halogen elements.

Naturally Aiba could never get to grips with technical terms of this kind. 'It boils down to this, the things called halogens, recently they have been found in the gas from Akadaké where they never were before. This professor's prediction of a coming big eruption for Akadaké is not at all surprising. That's what the article is all about.'

'The magazine . . . let me see it.'

Suda raised himself up on the bed and put out his hand to grasp what Aiba held out to him. Taka handed him his reading glasses. He slid the glasses down to the end of his nose and focused on the magazine, which he held with both hands, as though it were an object far away. 'Could the professor really be so hare-brained?' he wondered.

During the volcanic activity that created Mt Asama we made a chemical analysis of the gas issuing directly from the crater and also of the gas issuing from the hot springs in the Valley of Hades, about 3 kilometres from the crater. We then made a comparative study of the two emissions, trying to find some correlation between them. Our study confirmed that eruptions from the crater were invariably preceded by powerful emissions of foul smelling hydrogen sulphide . . .

Such was the beginning of Dr Maejima's article.

Furthermore, in the tenth year of Showa [AD 1935], on April 20, occurred an eruption previous to which a sample of gas from the crater mouth, after analysis, revealed the presence of methane in amounts well below normal, whereas the proportions of carbon monoxide and hydrogen ethane were

greatly increased. We further observed that consequent to
the eruption the proportions of ethane were still further
enhanced. Next, our recent review of available records on
Akadaké shows that the great eruption in the twelfth year of
Meiji [AD 1877] occurred at an altitude of 950 metres on the
western flank of the mountain. But at a point directly opposite
to the eruption, namely in an area at about 900 metres elevation on the eastern flank, the foul smell of hydrogen sulphide
was noticeable; furthermore, tests taken with glass tubing
inserted into the bowels of the earth at that time revealed
tremendous proportions of hydrogen ethane. Such phenomena do not occur without a cause. We have long been opposed
to the theory advanced by the late Dr Koriyama that Akadaké
is now a decrepit and extinct volcano. We wish to point out
that this mountain has the potential of erupting from either
flank. Because we anticipate that the next eruption of Akadaké will come from an area on the eastern flank at an elevation of 900 metres . . .

All the time Suda was reading, both Aiba and Taka were
nervously intent on observing the sick man's expression. By
and by Suda vigorously set to rubbing his face, which supported
the pair of spectacles on the end of his nose. The magazine slid
from his hand and fell to the floor.
  'How about it?' broke in Aiba with an uncontrived tense look
on his face. 'I didn't understand the article very well, but I
wasted no time in running here to the hospital.'
  'This magazine, where did you get it?'
  'From Sasaki, at the Hotel Fukuju.'
  Jinpei said nothing. He gazed at the ceiling. He was struggling
against the humiliation and the fear that he felt in his heart.
His pride was hurt. He himself and nobody else had made a
comprehensive study of Akadaké. Following the theory of Dr
Koriyama, it was he alone who had gone out to demonstrate
with his own two eyes, with his own two feet, that Akadaké
had little by little grown old and finally extinct. The hypothesis
in the magazine was nothing but a novelty, concocted by some
greenhorn scholar seated in his study and playing around in a

university with arguments based on little more than arbitrary logic. But a volcano is a living being. Mt Asama and Akadaké were identical neither in their geological formation nor in the nature of their eruptions. To say that what happened at Mt Asama was for such-and-such a reason, was no grounds at all for applying the same explanation to Akadaké.

Jinpei deliberately suppressed his inner misgivings. He took precautions against any display of resentment from his wounded pride. But he could not hide entirely the dark cloud of anxiety that spread within him.

'This isn't the first time. Ideas like this have been bandied about before.' He spoke with a quaver in his voice. 'Everybody wants to publish novel ideas.'

'In that case we're all set,' said Aiba, bobbing his head in satisfaction. He had been waiting for such reassurance from Suda. Nevertheless, he could not completely forget his own misgivings, and he added, 'But if the mountain does erupt, as the Professor says, it will wreck all my plans, won't it?'

Aiba's concern was not unreasonable. Dr Maejima had drawn attention to the fact that all through the history of Akadaké its volcanic activity was not restricted to only one spot on the occasions of its major eruptions. There was always simul-taneous activity on opposing sides of the mountain. The eruption in the Reign of Emperor Bunmei is a good example. On that occasion, at the very moment when boulders and dense black smoke blew skyward with an ear-splitting roar from an elevation of 820 metres on the south side, the north side too was active with an emission of blazing rocks from a ravine at the 800-metre level followed by overwhelming rivers of lava rolling down simul-taneously on the villages lying beneath either source.

Nevertheless, this usual twofold pattern of activity was un-explainably limited to only one side of the mountain in the most recent great eruption in the seventeenth year of Emperor Meiji. Consequently Dr Maejima, basing his opinion on the pattern of previous eruptions, was predicting that the next eruption would come from a point directly opposite to that of the Meiji Era eruption, in other words, near the 800-metre level somewhere on the eastern flank.

If Dr Maejima's prediction was on target, what could happen? The hamlets of Wari-ishi-zaki and Matsu-ura were safely on a direct line from the 800-metre level of the old eruption on the west flank of the mountain. But any overflow of lava from the centre of activity predicted by Maejima, would certainly pass straight through the site for which Aiba had drawn his plans to build the new hotel.

'Do you really think it's safe enough?'

'Look, it's safe, I tell you. Akadaké is impotent with old age.' Suda spoke softly but with firm conviction, letting his head sink back to the pillow.

'But listen, Suda San,' said Aiba, just to make double sure. He was picking up the magazine which had fallen to the floor. 'I have submitted the forms for a building permit, and I'm waiting for a decision. But if an idea like this magazine's should hit the local paper, I'm dead. We'll be in trouble. I'm really worried. So much so, I'm thinking I would have asked you yourself to take another look at the mountain, if only your health were better.'

Jinpei kept silent. He had definitely denied the possibility of another eruption, yet a vague, terrifying uncertainty still disturbed even him. Akadaké was not supposed to have another eruption. It could not erupt. But if another blow-up did occur, all the materials for his *History of the Eruptions of Akadaké*, which he had painstakingly amassed over fifteen years, month in and month out, would be worthless. All the energy he had expended in tramping over the mountain, ever since he had assumed his post at the local weather station – it would all be for nought. People had called him the Akadaké Demon. If only his health were better, there was no one more ready to charge the mountain again than Jinpei himself.

'I know it's out of the question, but maybe after a few weeks – for example, we could charter a cab, you know, and with the car it might be possible to get you up there. Suda San, what would you say to something like that?' It was typical of Aiba to be quite deferential when it suited his purpose.

'Anyway, the full-day sightseeing course runs up that far. I don't think the trip would be much of a strain on your condition.'

Jinpei gazed vacuously at Taka, who from her corner kept looking fitfully back and forth between her husband and the city councilman. Tense quiet settled on the sick-room. Through the wall they could hear the man next door furiously blowing his nose. It was that foreigner named Durand. With a glint in his eyes Aiba was watching for a reaction on Jinpei's face. But the wily city councilman, in view of the glum mood that had fallen on the room, decided for the moment not to press his point. He broke the tension with a hearty laugh.

'Let's forget it. I've been making demands that are quite unreasonable for anybody who's sick. Forget it, forget it.' He scratched his head vigorously then turned his apologies in Taka's direction. 'Mrs Suda, you have reason to be much put out with me.'

After Aiba's retreat, Jinpei remained motionless, stretched full length on the bed. He closed his eyes. Even he was shaken up, he, the man of self-assurance regarding Akadaké. Furthermore, what would be the attitude of a layman like Aiba? To which opinion would he naturally gravitate? To the opinion of a petty Surveillance Section Head at the local observatory? Or to that of a celebrated university professor? The answer was clear to Jinpei. The only reason the city councilman had for coming down on the side of Jinpei was that if he did not believe in Jinpei, his grandiose scheme for the new hotel was nothing but an iridescent bubble.

'Hey, Taka, come here.' With a trembling hand Jinpei beckoned for his wife. Assisted by Taka he rose from the bed and slowly made his way to the window. Across the bay Akadaké was raising towards the sky that single plume of smoke. The yellowish-brown slopes of the mountain lay in full view. The afternoon sun had painted one of the slopes in gold, making the surface puckers stand out one by one. 'It won't erupt,' he told himself. 'It won't erupt.'

On the following evening his elder son Ichiro came in unexpectedly on his way home from the office. Taka had already gone home, and Jinpei was all alone, lying on the hospital bed, turning over in his mind this and that about the ordeal of the day before.

'Dad, are you going to go to Akadaké in your condition? That's about what you'd expect from a guy like Aiba.'

Evidently he had heard about Aiba's visit from his mother. Ichiro sat in the chair, planting his legs on the edge of the bed. A cigarette dangled from his lips. He must have spent most of last night in a mah-jong parlour again, to judge from his washed-out colour. He was rubbing his scalp, which was flaky with dandruff, while he disguised his real intention behind a show of good-natured banter.

'In the first place, if your condition gets any worse, just think of the hospital costs. The retirement bonus will be gone before you know it.' Jinpei watched his face intently, remembering how Taka had complained that Ichiro was trying to get control of his father's nest egg. He had warned Taka to keep his personal seal away from Ichiro; but while he was in the hospital, Ichiro was likely now badgering, now wheedling his mother to hand it over. Without referring at all to that problem, Suda began to enquire about something else, about his son's wife.

'How is everything going, I mean with Sakiko?'

Since his admission to the hospital, his daughter-in-law had come to see him no more than three or four times. Taka was always full of complaints and disparaging comments about her. Jinpei himself felt no more affection or gratitude towards Sakiko than his wife did. Even when she did show up at the hospital, she never once offered to wash out her father-in-law's urine bottle. Dutifully she would sit there near the bed, but never once did she offer to relieve Taka in feeding him.

'You're wondering about Sakiko?' said Ichiro. His mouth was crammed with huge bites from the fruit which Aiba had left the day before. 'She's an awful, frigid woman; I'm beginning to think about separating. But most of all because Mother complains about her, too.'

When Jinpei heard these words, there crossed his mind once more that scene in the living-room, with images of the talisman and the dim light bulb, and the conversation between his son and his wife. But Jinpei could not bring himself to delve deeper into the meaning of what was sticking in his craw.

*   *   *

For the first time in two months Jinpei Suda left the hospital for an airing. On a pleasantly mild day close to the end of December they piled him into a taxi which Aiba had chartered. At first the staff physicians were adamantly set against the ill-advised outing, but when City Councilman Aiba applied pressure, and when the patient himself insisted on going at any risk, the doctors reluctantly gave permission, but only on condition that they include a trained nurse in the party.

In preparation for *Shogatsu*, the New Year holiday, the city enjoyed a bustling prosperity. There were pushcarts along the main street hawking traditional Shinto decorations of pinebranch sprays and loops of clean straw-plaited rope embellished with folded tufts of pure white paper. There was a line of street-stalls offering *kagami mochi*, the broad mirror-shaped cakes of pounded rice to place before the gods in household shrines. Here and there in the crowds could be seen pretty girls in brilliant kimonos, with their hair already dressed in elaborate geisha styles.

'*Shogatsu* is fun all right. The girls look more lovely than ever.' It was Aiba in his powerful voice, twisting around to speak from the front seat next to the driver. Jinpei sat in the back, scissored between his wife and the young nurse, who held a medical kit for his injections. Understandably he was feeling a bit light-headed from the exertion of moving about for the first time in weeks. He sat with eyes closed, with no comment more than a nod of the head in harmony with Aiba's monologue.

As they approached the waterfront district, the smell of the sea and of fish wafted into the car. The wind was blowing off the bay, and a forest of masts on the fishing boats filled the harbour. Men in rubberized mackintosh coats were busily loading cargoes of fish into waiting lorries.

The excursion boat doubled as a cargo ferry, an innovation for Japan at the time. They drove the taxi aboard with them for transportation on the island. Suda sat apathetically on a bench in the main cabin. The nurse stayed beside him. He was better than she had expected. She had worried about his arms and legs, but as he gradually got used to moving about, their action

seemed to be easier. Just as a precaution, however, she pinked
his right arm and injected a dose of tranquillizer.

There were very few passengers. Aiba typically went gadding
about to strike up a conversation with every familiar face among
the crew. From time to time he appeared in the cabin, wearing
his Inverness cape.

'Your colour is good. It's really good. You'll be all right,' he
called.

It was the same island Suda had known familiarly through the
years, but when they drew near the harbour of Shirahama, he
felt half like a stranger. Bright sunlight glinted off the lava rock
which covered the east side of the inlet. From a distance they
heard the usual scratchy record of popular music blaring a wel-
come to incoming passengers. Jinpei suddenly thought how he
himself would not be able to greet the New Year at home. He
would be in the hospital. It all seemed alien.

From the landing basin he was loaded into the taxi again. This
time Taka sat in front, and Aiba squeezed in the back with the
nurse, squashing Jinpei in the middle.

'I'm fine, all set,' said Jinpei.

But Aiba had a suggestion. 'Lean over by me. That way you'll
be more comfortable.'

Then Aiba cautioned the driver to move slowly as they
started up the sightseeing course, but even so splintered bits
of pumice stone pelted the underbody of the car. The steady
rat-a-tat sounded like beans popping in a roaster. The day was
abnormally warm for that part of December. The sky was
remarkably clear. The air was so pure that Akadaké's enormous
slopes glowed with the yellowish-brown colour of a fox, making
a contrasting background for the brilliant red in clumps of sumac
trees and for the great mounds of lava rock.

A trace of flaxen haze thinly veiled the higher peaks, but Suda
could not recall seeing the contours of the mountain standing
out in sharper focus than they did today.

'How could this peaceful mountain possibly explode?' he
thought when he opened his eyes from time to time and gazed
at the bright sky and the tranquil surface of the volcano. 'I

should have come immediately to inspect the mountain. I should not have been stopped by all that useless worry.'

Had the tranquillizer taken effect? At any rate the fear that had so preoccupied his mind gave way to euphoria. When he came to think of it now, that magazine article seemed pretty silly. If Akadaké were in fact unlimbering for an imminent blow, the seismographs maintained by the Observatory would certainly have recorded some tremors in the earth to be read as warning signs. There were no such tremors. It was reckless indeed to predict an eruption merely by the presence of increased amounts of certain gaseous compounds. 'Why was I upset about a case that even a layman could have decided?'

After a while, the car having executed a particularly sharp turn, there appeared a roadside marker indicating the 800-metre elevation. This was the point from which Akadaké was supposed to erupt, according to Dr Maejima.

On their left stood a clump of barren trees, and on their right a thick tangle of brush covered the steep sides of a rather deep ravine. The taxi squealed to a stop.

'Are you all right, Suda San?'

Aiba was out of the car first. He held out his hands, took hold of Jinpei's frame, and supported the full weight in his arms.

'You come with us, Nurse.'

Taka with her weak heart was feeling a little car-sick. Everyone agreed that she should stay in the taxi. Aiba and the nurse took turns in dragging Jinpei along the road that was littered with volcanic stones. A great part of the brush consisted of stunted pine tree growth, and a mixture of granite in the vicinity made for a whitish colour in the soil.

'There's no stinky smell around here.' Aiba was banging his *geta* to shake loose still another stone lodged between the cleats. 'The professor wrote about a lot of putrid smelling gas. I can't smell a thing. Let's score a point for Suda San,' Aiba said exuberantly.

It was true. In the clear mountain atmosphere there was not a trace of sulphur or the odour of any other gas that characterizes the atmosphere near the mouth of a volcano. Since there was scarcely any breeze, it was inconceivable that any ominous gas was being blown in a direction away from them. Perhaps the stench of hydrogen sulphide detected by Dr Maejima was in reality gas carried down from the crater mouth by an adverse wind on that particular day.

'After all the trouble of climbing the mountain, what do we have? Nothing. Suda San! I have to apologize.'

Aiba was out in front of the party, but he turned around and headed back. In his opinion they had nothing to gain by hiking any further.

Then Aiba noticed Jinpei pulling his arm away from the nurse and fixing his gaze intently at something on the ground.

'What did you find?' he asked, but Jinpei didn't answer. Aiba glanced down, and there was a black coloured object half-concealed in the shrubbery.

It was the remains of a field mouse.

The field mouse was dead. Its red mouth lay open to bare its rodent teeth. Its four extremities were fixed in rigor mortis, in a position like treading water. There was another remarkable circumstance. The shrubs of stunted pine in that particular spot were semi-withered. The pine needles were the colour of rust, as though they had been toasted. The whole area seemed pre-ternaturally quiet.

'Is that a field mouse?'

Aiba laughed. He turned towards the taxi and walked away.

All during their ride down the mountain, Suda rested against the nurse's shoulder. He kept his eyes closed. He didn't say a word. He saw branded in his mind's eye the detailed image of the field mouse carcass. The dead mouse was gruesome, dark red tongue extended, sharp teeth bared. A swarm of flies had begun to scrounge at the underbelly and on the rigid limbs.

He tried to expel the image, but the more he tried the more he became obsessed with the colour of that mouth and the contorted position of the four legs.

'It was nothing but a single mouse.' Jinpei was fighting back against the tumult in his soul. 'I suppose there's nothing to be afraid of.'

Nevertheless, if he had been a little more conscientious, if he had only looked a little further, he might have come across the remains of other mice and perhaps of other creatures. Why didn't he try to look further? Jinpei knew why he did not. He feared what he might find.

He had flinched in front of the field mouse because whenever a volcano shows any signs of unusual activity, the remains of dead spiders and little birds are often discovered on the ground. And sometimes trees begin to wilt, and occasionally creatures even as big as rabbits and field mice are affected. Sulphur gas leaking from the bowels of the volcano can poison the wild life.

For example, in the two months preceding the eruption of Mt Mihara in the fifteenth year of Showa (1940), vegetation began to wither here and there around the island village of Kamitsuki, and villagers found a number of dead sparrows and snakes.

There is another volcano in Hokkaido, called Usudaké, a mountain freshly created in the present Era of Showa. Along with the earth tremors and the cracks opening in the surface antecedent to the violent eruption, these same phenomena relating to wild life were observed in the vicinity of Fukuba, which today finds itself at the eastern foot of the new-made mountain.

Of course, merely because a field mouse had died there was no reason for leaping to the conclusion that sulphurous gas was breaking out. Nevertheless, it wasn't only the mouse. Why had the pine shrubs begun to wither? Why had the needles turned to a rust-colour, and only in that one area? The more he puzzled, the more that feeling of doubt and panic depressed his spirit. It was like a murky cloud pervading his soul.

'Akadaké will not play me false.' He opened his eyes and stole a look through the car window at the tawny mountain slopes. The sky was still as perfectly clear as it had been, and the white plume of smoke continued to rise slowly against the blue expanse. The spectacle was so brilliant that it pricked his eyes to look at it for long. He could not afford to lose his faith in Akadaké.

'How are you feeling now? Are you tired?' said Aiba, twisting around from the front seat.

'No, not so tired.'

'Even that university prof had it wrong.'

The city councilman's good spirits were completely restored. He reached a hand into the wide sleeve of his kimono and drew out a five-pack case of fat cigars. 'Mrs Suda,' he said, 'there wasn't enough sulphur there for one good silent fart.'

His jaunty quip for Taka was a stab in the groin to Suda.

'Best of all, this will finally convince Sasaki at the Hotel Fukuju. Don't you think so, Suda Kun?'

'I hope so.'

'It won't be long before we start the bulldozers rolling.'

Jinpei kept his eyes away from Aiba. He didn't only look away, he wanted to switch the topic of conversation, if he could. But all the way back to Shirahama, Aiba jabbered on incessantly about the methods to be used in levelling the ground, about the problems of how to sink the foundations.

Back at the hospital less than an hour later, Jinpei understandably felt exhausted. He lay perfectly motionless on the bed. He was turning over in his mind the problem of the mouse and the rust coloured pine needles.

'Yet there was not the slightest smell of gas,' he said to himself. 'Isn't that the best assurance?'

A psychological shock is the worst thing that can happen in Jinpei's kind of sickness. Nevertheless, on the following day, in spite of all that had occurred, he was still free of any ringing in the head or any sense of numbness in his body, long after he woke up. The doctor who came to take his blood pressure was obviously pleased at the reading.

'If this improvement holds,' he said, 'there won't be any problem about going home for *Shogatsu*. However, I caution you. Don't try anything as strenuous as what you did yesterday.'

Being talked to like this, Jinpei's spirits perked up, if only a little. It was encouraging to think that his health had improved enough to stand up against the emotional ordeal of the day before.

In the afternoon he made his way unaided down the corridor

to the nurse's station. It was to make a telephone call to the Observatory.

'Kinoshita Kun, is that you? Listen, please will you look something up for me?'

He asked his former underling to check the seismographic records for the last three or four days. Vibrations from Akadaké were picked up by portable equipment installed in little huts at various places on the mountain slopes beyond the town of Shirahama. Supposing anything unusual, it would be recorded with precision by agitated zigzags on the seismograph paper.

'My question is about the east flank. Has there been any special variation out that way?'

'Let me think.' Suda listened from over the wire to the knowledgeable voice of young Kinoshita.

'We haven't found any exceptional waves on the seismograms. The mountain has been absolutely quiet, I mean since the recent explosion.'

Jinpei put the telephone down. He breathed a sigh. It had all been the work of his timid imagination. Now he saw it clearly. Akadaké was, after all, the Akadaké that he had known it to be. Akadaké had not played him false. That being so, he also felt that he saw a way to explain the rust coloured withering of the pine-shrubs.

'I've got it! Why couldn't it be that a few volcanic stones came flying down as a result of that minor explosion?'

When you come to think about it, it was not inconceivable that the crater mouth on the mountain top had spewed some glowing cinders and hot stones that happened to land in the shrubbery here and there and scorched some of the stunted pine shrubs. He also hit on an explanation for the dead mouse: the mouse had not been asphyxiated, it had died a natural death.

As his health continued to improve, the doctor encouraged him to practise walking. The idea was to restore vitality to the legs, which had become thin and flabby, not only as a direct result of his stroke, but also because he had stayed in bed for so long. With his aged wife at his side, he took to moving back and forth along the corridor, one step at a time, and then up and down the stairs. It became a routine. Every day he paused to study Akadaké from the window by the end of the corridor. He gazed at the sea that glittered in the winter sunlight. He scanned the city which had been his home for fifteen years.

Once he was released from the hospital he could finally begin to organize his *History of the Eruptions of Akadaké*. He revived the dream of spending his remaining years in that fond task. On the evening of a day spent thus, Jinpei happened to come abreast of the old foreigner, who like himself was gazing at Akadaké from the corridor window. The old man had draped a threadbare overcoat over his frowzy dressing robe. He wiped his nose repeatedly with a handkerchief, while his gaze was bent on eating into the gloomy mist that now enveloped the volcano.

'That's the foreign gentleman in the room next to yours,' Taka whispered softly to Jinpei, making her reference doubly clear with a roll of her eyes in the foreigner's direction.

But the man with the name that sounded like Durand or something, stood there motionless, his weight resting on one leg, his face pressed against the window.

'It's getting colder, don't you think?'

Jinpei took the occasion to ingratiate himself with a friendly exchange of greetings. At the sound of his voice, the foreigner turned to face him. Jinpei observed that the eyes were foreigner's big round eyes were gleaming with what seemed to be tears.

SIX

It was of no interest to people like Jinpei and Taka, but today was the day before Christmas.

The flapping sounds of their loose slippers gradually faded far to the other end of the now dim corridor. Durand listened, his face against the window. He returned to his room, wiping his eyes and nose with the dirty handkerchief. The room was cold. The metal frame of the hospital bed reflected cheerless glints in the twilight. Dirty dishes lay scattered on the table. The milky white of evening fog was beginning to paint the windows.

'Sacré vieux chien . . . Sacré vieux chien.' Durand sat in a kind of daze on the edge of his bed, mumbling his old incantation while he gently massaged his aching legs. From down the corridor he heard the piercing squeal of the toilet door. There was not another sound on the whole second-floor ward. This particular hour, and the long night hours following, were the hardest part of the day. The scabs on his old wounds were again picked open, and the memory of each different wound raised its gorge to his throat.

Gradually the room became completely dark, but he never gave a thought to turning on a light. When he first came to live in the hospital, being left alone in the room seemed intolerable. As twilight settled in, he invariably turned on the switch, to cheer up body and soul. But a glaring light bulb wasn't any help.

To tell the truth, the doctor had given him special permission to go out on this particular day, the first such permission in a long while. Christmas was no great thing for Durand, but one of the younger doctors – one who was not aware of Durand's past – had said to him with the kindest intent, 'I know it's a special day for our foreign residents,' and he wrote out the pass.

If Durand did leave the hospital, he had nowhere to go, no one to visit. Now he lay stretched full length on the bed, eyes open vacuously in the dark. Memories began their prowl, up from the subconscious, like phantoms from the past. It was heart-wrenching. From his old suitcase under the bed he took out the black clothes which he had not even touched for so long. He looked them over, listlessly.

As he presented the gate pass at the front desk of the hospital, the woman in charge of the footwear lockers was sitting at the *hibachi* warming her hands.

'Hello, Durand San. It's Christmas. Are you going out to church?' She displayed her jutting red gums in a big smile. 'Christmas for you foreigners is like New Year's for us Japanese, don't you think?'

The night was cold enough to chill the bones. He followed the wall of the hospital in the pitch dark, making his way to the bus stop. Was it because he had not been outside for so long? His rheumatic legs began to ache more than ever.

'What good does it do to go out?' is what he was thinking, but when a bus going to the Hataya-cho business section came along, he got aboard.

'Where to, please?'

The young girl-conductor, face red with the cold, came over to him and he replied, 'Kurato-cho.'

Why Kurato-cho? He was not aware of any obvious reason for mumbling the name of that particular stop. Kurato-cho was the address of the church where Father Ginzo Sato was pastor. It was the Feast of the Nativity. Probably the Christians were not yet all assembled to assist at Midnight Mass. The only ones to show up this early would be the ones who wanted to go to confession. How would they react if they saw Durand? No one could answer that one better than Durand himself. Moreover, he anticipated the look on the face of Ginzo Sato when the priest met him, a look ambivalent with pity and contempt. Pretending to be not at all surprised, the priest would lead Durand quickly and unobtrusively into his private room in the rectory.

Durand blew his nose in the handkerchief, while his whole body continued to vibrate with the rattle of the bus. It seemed that he had an actual prevision of the reception awaiting him at the church in Kurato-cho.

Along with that – again he knew not why – there came a feeling of punishing pleasure in imagining how he was about to expose himself to looks of contempt and rejection. He was casting aside all self-respect, he was spitting in his own face. Durand secretly took pleasure in his black expectations.

'So I'm on my way to the church, that's for sure.'

He settled it within, and outwardly he arranged his mouth in a thin smile.

Kurato-cho is in the oldest part of the city. In a bygone age it had been the neighbourhood for Samurai of modest means. The whole area had burned out during the war. Now the streets were lined with small shops. The church compound stood at the edge of the business section, where the street lights ended abruptly in darkness.

When he got off the bus, the wooden cross on the church hovered in the dark above the house tops. In front of the gate to the compound he saw two or three boys, apparently junior high school age, straddling their bicycles and talking together. They didn't seem to know Durand, but even so they dropped their conversation and looked him over curiously.

'Father is in the chapel, I suppose?'

'Who knows?' one of the boys answered with a touch of derision. 'None of us belong to the "Amens".'

Durand walked past, and sniggers broke out behind his back.

Seeing nobody near the door of the chapel, he felt relieved. He raised his scarf to mask the lower half of his face before sliding open the door of the priest's house. An aroma like that of butter tickled his nose. The smell was emanating from the kitchen and mixing with the stuffy air of the heated house. The tidy hallway, the holy pictures on the wall, the bouquet of ample food. For the first time these impressions revived the memory of life in a priest's house, the way of life which he had left behind long ago.

Father Sato's room lay at the end of the hallway. Durand

placed his cane in the umbrella rack and started softly down the hall. His legs began to ache again – because he had not been out for so long?

A faint halo of light was seeping out from around the door frame.

'Is somebody there?'

The recognizable voice of Father Sato came from inside the room.

'If you want confession, wait in the chapel.' It was character- istic of priests, that tone of voice like a superior giving orders to inferiors. There had been occasions in the old days when he himself had talked that way to the faithful.

In the glow of a table lamp Father Sato was arranging a cassock on his well-fleshed frame. He was facing the other way, towards a four-eyed schoolboy, and he did not immediately notice that it was Durand in the doorway.

'My gosh is it *you*?' he suddenly blurted, his ruddy face betraying for the moment a mixture of shock and embar- rassment.

'You're surprised, aren't you, Sato San?'

'No, not at all, but . . . What in the world brings you out at this time?'

'Only for a change of pace. Just as you see, I came from the hospital only for a social visit.'

Even in the presence of the schoolboy Durand made a point of addressing the priest not with the title of *Shinpu* ('Father') but with the over-familiar title of *San* ('Mister').

'If I am disturbing you, please say so. I used to be a priest too, so I appreciate how busy you must be on Christmas Eve.'

Father Sato was upset. He stole a quick glance at the student. For the priest personally it didn't matter so much; but for Dur- and in the presence of a schoolboy, to reveal so off-handedly that he was an ex-priest – it disturbed Sato's sense of clerical dignity.

'I'll see you in a minute . . . ,' said the priest, dismissing the student with a gesture. Was this four-eyed boy really sharp enough to catch the situation? At any rate, he bobbed his head and shoulders, but only towards Father Sato, and keeping his eyes away from Durand, he made his escape.

'So you have another prospect, do you? I mean that kid. The Church in Japan is as active as ever.'

'That's right.' Father Sato, unmindful of Durand's ironic smile, readily agreed. 'The young students especially are increasing again. That boy is only one of the group for baptism next year.'

Hearing this, Durand blinked his eyes. He didn't know why, but right then and there he caught a vision of the tight, drawn face of Dr Tsugawa on the day he baptized her.

For a while neither of them said a word. The gas stove in a corner of the room blazed away with a noisy rasp. Durand had his own memories of this particular eight-*tatami* room. Around the time when he was pastor at Sakai-machi, a priest from Canada had been living here.

'Won't you have an apple or something?'

A basket of fruit tied in ribbon was resting on Father Sato's table, no doubt a gift which one of the faithful had brought for the Christmas festivities. However, Father Sato made no particular move to untie the ribbon. The invitation was no more than a conventional phrase to fill the awkward gap in the conversation.

'How are you getting along, Durand San? How is your health?'

The gas stove continued its dry, hissing sound.

Durand turned his back and wiped his face with the dirty handkerchief. He was painfully aware that the priest was anxious to be rid of him in a hurry. But Durand felt a childish delight in irritating the priest by deliberately behaving in just the opposite way to what the priest so obviously wanted.

'Well, well! Look at the blueprints!' whooped Durand, walking over to a wall on which were pinned some building plans.

'I am thinking of setting up a retreat house for the Christians at the foot of Akadaké.

Unaware of the trap being laid by Durand, Father Sato rushed to explain. 'I have the bishop's permission, so the only problem left is the actual construction. Anyway, I think I mentioned this to you before at some time or other.'

The white lines of the blueprint showed the design of a two-storeyed Japanese-style house, and along one edge of the paper were inscribed characters spelling out *St Theresa's Villa*.

'You have a chapel. You have a dining-room. You even have an assembly hall,' observed Durand, smiling sarcastically and keeping his back turned towards the priest. 'How big is the site?'

'A little more than 400 *tsubo*.'

'Sato San, Akadaké is safe, you think?'

'What do you mean?'

'Akadaké exploded again lately, exactly the way that I predicted it would the last time I saw you, and . . .'

'That was only a momentary disturbance. As for being safe enough, even the Observatory guarantees it.'

'You're so right, Sato San.'

'Let's agree to drop that subject for tonight, shall we?'

To keep Durand from saying any more, the priest himself lapsed into silence, while his hands played with the basket of fruit on the table.

Durand studied the chubby, slumped down figure of the priest with anger and resentment. That dish-like face, smooth and rosy-cheeked. Eyes like those of a peasant farmer, eyes that had never once in their whole life been shocked by a penetrating look at the murky things deep inside himself. Like everything in the room, like everything in the house, his life was primly arranged in proper order. Father Sato was smugly confident that he would always live true to the faith, completely at peace with himself.

'Durand San, I am busy today. For one thing, the Christians are waiting in the chapel now for confession.' His plump fingers kept playing with the basket of fruit. Every fibre in his frame abhorred Durand.

Acting against his aversion, and because Durand kept standing there mutely, the priest opened a drawer, reached in, and without looking up, said, 'Here, Durand San.'

'What is it?'

'Please take it. A little Christmas present from me.'

There were two packs of cigarettes and a folded thousand yen note. Durand watched the priest's face intently for a moment. Then he smiled the thin, sardonic smile and extended his hand.

When he got outside the house, stars were glowing in the jet black sky. From within the chapel came the tones of the wheezy organ, playing along for the young people practising hymns for Midnight Mass. When the chorus broke down, they started off again from the beginning.

Slipping his fingers into his pocket, Durand put a firm grip on the money and the cigarettes he had just been favoured with. He recalled the look of relief in the eyes of Father Sato at the moment he handed them over. Of course, Durand's hand had been a little shaky when he took the cigarettes and the money. But he sensed that painful pleasurable feeling in playing the role of panhandler, in throwing away his self-respect in the face of the other's contemptuous pity.

'I'll do something still more dirty.'

Durand moved towards the chapel. Two women of the parish stood chatting in front of the door. They caught sight of Durand shuffling along on his cane, and jerked back to clear the way. As he walked past, something like a sharp pain shot through his chest. He was not surprised.

Tones came from the reedy organ, but the instrument needed oil. Five or six men and women were standing there with their eyes fixed on the music in their hands.

'Starting right from there, once more now.'

Waving her hands like a regular conductor, a middle-aged woman cued them in, and off they went again.

> Glory to God in the highest,
> Lord and Saviour, Which art in heaven;
> Thou art the King of Israel,
> Lord of Heaven and Earth,
> Offshoot of David, and Lord or Lords.

Suddenly the voices stopped, but the organ went on, slowed in tempo. Durand was dragging his feet forward in the chapel.

He stopped. The organ stopped. Behind his back Durand felt the gaze of the Christians waiting for confession, the gaze of the young men and women practising hymns. He deliberately fixed a smile on his face. He took his time, indulging that aching pleasurable feeling.

Somebody went 'Sh-h-h!' There was whispering going on behind him. Durand knew that somewhere in the chapel was the student who had been in Father Sato's room earlier on.

'What's the matter with all of you?'

Durand abruptly turned to face them. They stared at him with timid, sober smiles. He met them all with a smile.

'Please continue singing.'

He had recognized the woman playing the organ. Dressed in kimono, wearing glasses, no doubt about it, she was a woman who had belonged to his parish eight years before.

'I'll do something still more dirty . . . something still more dirty.' Close to his ear a kind of voice kept repeating it, rhythmically. Durand took a tight grip on the cigarettes and the folded money in his pocket.

'Kiga San!'

Smiling, he called to the woman seated at the organ.

'Remember me?'

When she made no answer, he said in a louder voice, 'My name is Durand. I baptized you.'

A clatter of agitated footwear came from the entrance vestibule, and even inside the chapel they heard a voice appealing for help.

'Please, Father Sato.'

'What's the trouble?'

Father Ginzo Sato took a look inside. He caught sight of Durand and let out a low-keyed yelp.

'Durand San!' His voice was urgent and harsh. 'Come out here, please.'

'For what, Sato San?'

Emotion surged. Durand went livid with rage. He wanted to destroy the whole place – church furnishings, the organ, the faces of the Christians huddled in the corner, their eyes fascinated by the horror of him – all these he wanted to shake up, slash, smash to smithereens.

'Is it forbidden for me to be here, Sato San?'

'Not exactly forbidden, but . . .'

'Every man has a right to enter a church, does he not? I am not exactly one of those money changers driven out by Christ.'

'No, you are not, but . . .'

When Durand started to move, the Christians in the corner shifted their own position inch by inch.

Father Sato was standing by the wall near the entrance, his face flushed red, his eyes begging Durand to leave. His fatty flesh quivered.

'The likes of you will never fathom my misery, but this misery of mine . . .' Durand kept his mouth shut, however, suppressing any further speech along those lines. As for the words he had already spoken, there was no way to recall them.

In a moment his feelings changed to a sense of utter lassitude and futility. It was the collapse that follows any orgasmic pleasure.

Keeping his face averted, Durand got past Father Sato and made it outside.

'I'm sorry,' said Father Sato, as though whispering into Durand's ear. 'I don't mind having you come to the church. But it shocks the Christians. And makes for neighbourhood gossip. Please try to understand.'

Durand walked in a daze to the bus stop. It dawned on him that he had left his cane in the vestibule of the church. It annoyed him.

Shops in these outlying districts close down early. There was no other sound in the hushed street but his own dragging footsteps. Reaching the bus stop, he leaned on the sign post for a little, eating his heart out, chilled to the marrow.

Long, long ago, he himself on this same night had offered Mass in a church, delivered the sermon, and joined with the faithful in the give and receive of celebrating Christmas. It was very long ago; and besides that, the priest who had done these things was not at all like this man Durand.

He had been free of cardiac pain for a while, but all of a

sudden a seizure racked his chest. He searched his pockets for his medicine, but the only thing his fingers reached were the cigarettes from Father Sato. He held on to the sign post, waiting motionless for the seizure to pass.

'*Sacré vieux chien . . . sacré vieux chien.*' He closed his eyes and went on mumbling.

'*Sacré vieux chien . . .*'

SEVEN

Jinpei Suda had the doctor's permission to go home for the three days of *Shogatsu*. His progress had been favourable. The paralysis in his arm and leg had been eased notably, and lately he could even navigate up and down the stairs without the help of his wife or a nurse. Even his tongue, which had been utterly inarticulate, was able to function again, though his speech was tantalizingly slow.

It was warm in the late afternoon of the final day of the old year. At New Year there was rarely any snow in this city located in southern Japan, but Jinpei thought that a day unseasonably mild like today could be followed by rain or even snow. He was sitting up in bed, flipping the pages of a newspaper that he had read through several times already, waiting for his wife Taka to pick him up. The door finally opened, and framed in the door stood, much to his surprise, his daughter-in-law Sakiko.

Sakiko hesitated a moment as though looking at something indecent. She frowned at the urine bottle wrapped in paper on the floor, at the dishes and the fruit peelings scattered on the table.

'The car is waiting downstairs.'

Then she cut him, withdrawing to the corridor where she would bide her time until her father-in-law emerged. She made no effort to help him out of his bed clothes and into his business suit. Putting on his socks was quite a struggle for him.

Since he had entered the hospital, Sakiko did well if she came to see him once a week. Even then she never lent a hand in feeding him, much less did she offer to relieve Taka of the dirty job of rinsing out the urine flask or anything of that kind. As for Taka, she herself had never ceased complaining about Sakiko.

Just because Sakiko had had the advantage of going to college
– Sakiko had eventually managed to graduate from some provincial finishing school – she was stuck up, she had no respect
whatsoever for old folks like themselves. Suda didn't say anything to Taka, but he too had no cause for satisfaction in their
daughter-in-law.

When the mini-cab, after its long wait, slipped away from the
hospital entrance, Jinpei on the spur of the moment enquired
about his son Ichiro. He happened to think of all the gripes he
heard against Sakiko whenever Ichiro showed up at the hospital.
More than once Ichiro had muttered, spitting out the words,
'Dad, I feel like separating from a frigid woman like her. What
the hell . . .'

Sakiko squeezed as close as possible to her own side of the
car, avoiding any body contact with her father-in-law. She kept
watching the tinselled lights along the street, and without turning her head she answered, 'Ichiro? Who knows where he is?
Probably at a year-end party somewhere. He'll be home late.'

Clearly she felt no concern, no interest, in her husband's
doings. While he furtively peeked at her in profile, Jinpei saw
the jutting cheekbones and the rather cross expression, and he
thought that the disparaging comments of Taka and Ichiro were
justified. But beyond that, he did not intend to get involved in
trouble between Ichiro and Sakiko. He had always followed a
policy of peace at any price. The only thing he dreaded in the
extreme was that discord in the family might affect himself. It
was always thus with Jinpei, he was far more preoccupied with
keeping up appearances than with the feelings of his wife or son
or daughter-in-law. How the daughter-in-law might feel about
his son was for him of minor import. What threatened him was
that if by any chance the couple did break up, their falling out
would sow the seeds of gossip touching on himself and Taka.
Life in a small provincial city was not like living in Tokyo. When
word got out about the daughter-in-law of that former Section
Head in the Weather Bureau – that she bolted the barnyard –
the people who knew him would need a long time to exhaust
that titillating topic.

Within half an hour Jinpei was home again, yet at first it all

seemed strange. Understandably so. He felt he had been out
of circulation for ages, although in fact he had been in the hospital barely two months. Having exchanged his business suit for
a brand new padded kimono which Taka had stitched for him,
he sat down cross-legged in the living-room. The surroundings
suddenly brought to mind the sequence of events in the long
night after his collapse, how he had been brought by car from
the Eiraku Inn, how he had first been put to bed in this same
living-room. Remaining in his memory from the moment that
he came to his senses were these identical faded spots on the
ceiling, this clock hanging on the wall, the Shinto talisman pinned
to the vertical house post to ward off fire.

And then the exchange of talk between Ichiro and Taka as
they sat beside his floor bed. It seemed that he could hear it
again close to his ear.

'Mother, you have resented the Old Man for a long time,
even if he never guessed it.'

'What are you driving at?'

'All right . . . but it's obvious to me.'

What was it that was obvious to Ichiro? What was it that Taka
resented? In the hospital he had been on the point of asking
Taka and Ichiro about this conversation. It wasn't that he'd
never had a chance to broach the subject, but in the end he had
never dared to bring it up. Why not? Because he was afraid to
interrogate his wife and son. In his own mind, of course, he
never could find a reason for Taka to resent him. He admitted
that after their wedding he had not been a paragon of a husband.
Now and then, when they were young, he had walloped her and
booted her in the behind, but they all did it back in those days.
One thing though, he never had the grit, or the extra money
required, for messing with other women. He never even
dreamed of setting up a love nest, or of staking out exclusive
claim on any one loose woman. From that angle, as a husband
he was not so bad.

'That's the way things were . . . and from now on I don't
intend to make a mountain of a molehill, prying into anything
like that.'

Having so resolved, Jinpei then became desperately euphoric

for the remainder of the evening. He was happy to sit at table
with his family after the long separation. He had his younger
son, the junior high school boy, sitting next to him, for Ichiro
was not yet home.

'The food at the hospital is vile. It's good to be home, I tell
you, good to be home.' Jinpei was bobbing his head, displaying
his satisfaction.

'You know, I really did have it bad, but somehow or other I
feel better now. I can live the rest of my days in peace.'

With spectacles sliding down his nose, he turned to address
himself to his younger son Kenjiro, who at that moment was
raking his rice bowl with his chopsticks.

'How is school? Always keep working for good marks, and
grow up to be a man who will always command respect.'

Before his illness, it had been his custom every night at
dinner, while he sipped at his half-pint of *sake*, to speak to his
son of practical maxims for success in life. But *sake* was now
forbidden. He waved his chopsticks instead of a bottle, to
restart the schoolboy sermon broken off two months before.
But Kenjiro failed to react. Keeping the rice bowl close to his
chin he showed no sign of anything except an excellent appetite.

'In my opinion . . . the best for a man is the golden mean. It
spells out happiness.'

At this point he was addressing no one in particular, but he
murmured the words with profound emotion. Then he happened
to glance at Sakiko, who was sitting next to Jiro. She had been
silent, with her eyes cast down, when unexpectedly she raised
her face to Jinpei. It lasted no more than a moment, but Jinpei
caught the contemptuous smirk, the cynical twist to her lips.

Jinpei's sleep was interrupted by the call of nature. It was past
midnight when he awoke. Immediately he recollected how he
had stayed in the living-room until about ten o'clock, listening
to the radio – a song festival bidding farewell to the old year,
along with other entertainments. Was it the sudden change in
his routine? Not surprisingly he had felt tired, and he had asked
Taka to spread the quilts. Then he had gone to bed.

'It must be New Year's Day by now.'

Every year invariably he would wait to listen for the temple bells. He regretted having fallen asleep so early this year – blame it on his illness. With the turn of midnight he became sixty years of age, according to the method of counting used in Japan. Taka was snoring next to him in bed. He called her softly, wanting her to fetch the urinal, but the good wife failed even to roll over in sleep.

Jinpei got to his feet. He groped along the wall, fumbling for the sliding panel that would open onto the corridor. He was disorientated. Because he had been away so long? He couldn't for the life of him find the way out.

The toilet was at the far end of the corridor. Feeling his way along the wall, Jinpei proceeded slowly. Loosely he held a front hem of his sleeping-kimono, hanging open to his naked front. There was still a light in the room of Ichiro and Sakiko, providing a gleam in that part of the corridor. Jinpei overheard the couple talking together. He thought of the glimpse he had caught last night of Sakiko's disdainful glance in his direction.

'What about the money for hospital bills and for therapy?'

It was Sakiko's voice.

'Mother's not likely to ask for any money from the two of us.'

'But we didn't know that the Old Man was going to use his retirement bonus to pay the bills.'

Silence for a while. Jinpei held to the night-cold wall, ears cocked to catch the next words.

'I won't have it. I won't! The same thing over again. I can't stand going back to living like we were. Did you think Dad would get well? I thought he wouldn't.'

'If I did think so, it wasn't up to me to say anything.' Sakiko spat the words of her objection, which combined with the dry sibilation of the quilts rubbing together as she settled into the bedding.

'If only he had dropped dead on the spot, the whole retire-ment bonus would have come to us intact. That's why I have no use for old people. They're a bunch of freeloaders. As long as they live, they never cotton on to how everybody resents them.'

'How does Mother feel about it?'

'Same as us, I'm pretty sure. When Dad was stricken, the one that really felt relieved was Mum.' He punctuated his opinion with a tongue click. 'But the old bore is home again. Crap!'

The bedroom light went out. A dog howled somewhere far away. When the howling died, a cheerless hush fell on the house. Jinpei leaned against the wall, holding his breath. Then he groped his way back, the same way he had come. He got past Taka without kicking her bedding then squatted down on his own bed. He sat there staring at the dark.

One by one the words he had overheard from his married children convulsed the inner membrane of his ear.

'Ichiro and Sakiko . . . and even Taka.'

Jinpei never entertained the thought that his wife and children idolized their father. Being in love and being loved were empty words to his old age. Nevertheless, he had mistily imagined to himself the scene around his death bed – Taka moistening his lips with a final sip of water, his son and his son's young wife dropping an honest tear in grief for him. He never dreamed that in the pre-dawn of that very *Shogatsu* marking the advent of his sixtieth year, he would be shut out in the cold by his family, his own flesh and blood.

Jinpei's eyes were glowing in the dark. He heard the wind rustle through the garden. He couldn't believe that the words of his son and daughter-in-law were true. Somewhere far away the dog was baying again. One night in the hospital he had suddenly woken up at the hacking cough from that foreigner in the next room. He couldn't get back to sleep that night, and had lain in the dark and listened to the wind. It was like tonight, except that in the hospital he had had an early final release, the impending visit home for *Shogatsu*, and things like that to look forward to.

'I did come home, did I not?'

Dazedly he turned his eyes to the side. His wife was snoring. Spontaneously he made to call her name, but closed his mouth again. He recalled how once, long ago, he had been touched at reading of the sadness of an old man who never laid his hand

on the body of his wife except to stop her snoring. Jinpei's case
was even sadder, for Jinpei could no longer even reach his wife.
Despite their being two in one flesh through many years, they
were strangers to each other after all. Loneliness suffused him,
and it ached.

The first day of the New Year dawned beneath a leaden sky
that Jinpei imagined might bring snow. He washed his face in
the first water he drew from the tap.*

Moving to the living-room he saw laid out on the table the
dovetailed stack of lacquered boxes (bargain basement quality)
full of holiday goodies. He saw the service for drinking *toso*.
Taka was crouching by the *hibachi* and toasting *mochi*. Without
really thinking what he was doing, Jinpei kept his eyes on where
he was stepping to get past Taka.

She looked up and said, 'Won't you write our names on the
chopstick holders?'

'All right.'

On the first day of the year the head of the house writes the
names of the members of the family on the sheaths in which
they keep their chopsticks. It was a custom in those parts.
Picking the raddled writing brush from the inkstone box, Suda's
rather shaky hand drew his own name, then Taka's name, then
the names of his sons, and finally that of his daughter-in-law. In
former years Jinpei had always found a puerile sort of happy
exhilaration in this function that symbolized his being master of
the household. Mixed in his feelings was the profound satisfaction that without benefit of a college education he had risen to
the rank of Section Head in the local weather bureau, a status
that commanded respect. This year, however, as he plied the
writing brush, he was thinking of what had happened in that
early pre-dawn hour. He had no control of the brush, the character strokes were wobbly.

The members of the family took their regular places around
the low table. Was Ichiro going out for his round of New Year

* By tradition the first water drawn on New Year's Day had preternatural
power to cleanse from evil.

calls? He wore a new suit, which Jinpei had not seen before. Ichiro sat down, taking off his jacket.

'Well, Dad, pour me some *toso*, please.'

Sakiko was next to her husband. She too was dressed for going out. When Jinpei poured *toso* into the cup held out by Ichiro, his hand shook uncontrollably. This man Ichiro, who looked at him now with a grin, was the very man who had said those words, 'If only he had dropped dead on the spot, the whole retirement bonus would have come to us intact.'

'Won't Mum have a drink too?'

'I can't drink. I'll take a tiny cup, just to be polite.'

Taka presented her tiny cup in both tiny hands for her husband to fill. In honour of the holiday she had removed from the collar of her kimono the sweat band which had borne the grease of the departed year.

'This woman has no reason for thinking that way . . . those things about me . . .' Jinpei stole a glance at his wife. Taka put her cup down on the table and turned to serve the bowls of *zoni*.

'It's wonderful you recovered so fast that you can celebrate New Year's at home,' she said, but then she suddenly looked surprised. 'What's wrong? You look so pale.'

'It's nothing.'

Jinpei shook his head in annoyance. He had been trying to make a show of being enormously pleased at getting out of hospital, yet he was fully aware that each of them at the table entertained their own unspoken thoughts. He caught Sakiko glancing at him again with that belittling smirk on her face, the same sardonic turn to her lips that he had seen at table last night.

After the festive bowl of *zoni*, the family left the house, one after another. Ichiro and Sakiko were to visit Sakiko's family, who lived in Kawamachi. Kenjiro, the younger son, was to pay his respects at the home of his junior high school teacher. Only Taka remained, darting back and forth between the kitchen and the living-room. Having settled himself into the *kotatsu*, Jinpei kept his eye on the tiny figure of Taka bobbing in and out of the kitchen. The radio carried a programme of sombre court music of ancient times direct from the Imperial Palace. From outside the house he heard the piping voices of children playing shuttlecock.

'Nothing has changed,' he thought. 'Nothing changed.' But even so, he began to feel that this was not the same as the morning of *Shogatsu* the year before. He couldn't lay his finger on what was different, but the difference provoked a gelid sense of isolation that settled in the marrow of his soul.

'Hey, Taka!'

In a pleading tone, Jinpei raised his voice. 'Taka . . . please!'

'What is it?'

'Taka, you said something . . . that night . . .' But then he closed his mouth, as though swallowing his heartburn. 'It's nothing . . . I'm going to visit the Observatory.'

'The Observatory! Nobody's there today.'

Nevertheless, without further ado, he removed his padded kimono. Normally Jinpei demanded personal service, never lifting a finger to help himself, but today he laid out his business suit all on his own.

Taka stoutly objected to her husband's going out. He was not yet fully recovered. But without a word in reply, he went. A bright sun was finally beginning to penetrate the haze. It was more like New Year's ought to be. He had no luck trying to hail a cab, but he could easily go directly to the Observatory from the bus stop near his house. The bus was loaded with family groups, some of the men already flushed crimson from too much *toso*. A teenage lad, seeing Jinpei struggle to keep his footing, politely offered him a seat. Right next to Jinpei was a five- or six-year-old with a picture book. The book was open and the boy was asking his mother a question. The picture book was about King Lear.

Jinpei had little contact with the likes of Shakespeare, but he was familiar with the story of Lear. His son Ichiro, while still in elementary school, had once declaimed a passage from *Lear* for his part in class-day exercises. Jinpei knew that the tale concerned a man deserted by his daughters. That's all he knew, yet under present circumstances he felt self-conscious about it.

He left the bus in front of the Weather Bureau. The building

in which he had worked for so many years stood silent as the
grave. Some boys were playing in the quadrangle. He stepped
into the entrance way, where a few of the footwear lockers
were broken as they had always been. He smelt the indoor
privy, he smelt the dust from the corridor. The hanging map of
Japan, the water stains on the wall – nothing had changed from
his working days. Jinpei closed his eyes and stood there filling
his lungs with odours of nostalgia.

'You're the Section Chief, aren't you?' somebody called to
him. He turned to find the old janitor, who lived with his wife
in a tiny house close to the main building.

Jinpei ripped his face in a smile. 'Hello there. I happened to
be passing by. Is there no one here on holiday duty?'

'Kato San's in charge today, but he just went home for lunch.
Good to see you, Chief. How's your health?'

The janitor was convivial. He was dangling a water kettle
from one hand.

'No problems. But I'm no longer a "chief". I . . . uh-h . . .
is it all right to visit the Surveillance Section office?'

He started up the stairs, but stopped. He asked the janitor,
'You had a son, did you not?'

'Yes, an only boy.'

He looked intently down at the janitor. Jinpei had never made
plans to meet the problem of age, but the problem came home
to him again in the image of this old man. The hard necessity
of continuing to live after a man grows old. He had never anticipated the sadness of it, but the sadness touched his heart again
where it hurt.

He walked into the office of the Surveillance Section. Here
too everything was familiar. After his retirement, his second in
command, Mr Nakamura, had moved up to Section Head. The
desk and the chair that Suda had used were still set close to
the window sill. The shelves of record books stood in their
regular places. Affectionately Jinpei rubbed his hand along the
shelves. Then he eased his way into the chair and turned his
face to Akadaké visible in the distance.

The mountain still hid its upper half in the clouds as it had been doing, and exposed its slopes and darkish foot through a haze.

'Only the mountain does not betray me.'

It was because of what had happened last night that this sombre emotion swept the heart of Jinpei. He was loath to say it, but the fact remained that he considered the mountain to be the only one deserving his trust. Because the mountain too had grown old in sympathy with him. He blinked his eyes and gazed forever at the ugly wrinkles on the decrepit volcano, the dark grey of the hazy mountain foot. Never before had the mountain so perfectly mirrored the loneliness and the isolation in his own heart. No doubt it was simply because he had never been so utterly obsessed with lonely depression as he had since the night before. Akadaké moved in rhythm to match his heart. As he grew old, the mountain too went senile.

He drew several volumes of records from the shelf and turned the pages with reverential care. Every sheet represented the fruit of his own investigations and his own careful compilations during the active years. Yet none of the data was his personal property. He had even lost the right to consult the materials.

Mr Kato had still not come back. Most likely in going home for lunch he seized the occasion to forget his job, going off for a New Year's visit somewhere.

As Jinpei left the Surveillance Section room, he turned around to gaze once more at Akadaké through the windows. He thought he might never again have a chance to see the volcano from here. Then going down the stairs, he could find on the ground floor no trace of even the janitor. Although he had no particular business going down still lower, he wanted only to have a look into the seismological laboratory in the basement. When he got to the lower level, it was dark and musty. From behind the laboratory door he could hear the drone of the motor. The smell of the cement and the faint beat of the mechanism brought back the fondest of memories. He felt that just to fill his lungs in this nostalgic atmosphere would miraculously help to clear his head of the Ichiro business, the Sakiko business, and all the business of the talk which he had overheard last night.

The seismograph was functioning in ruffled clitter clatter. The slightest shake from Akadaké or from the bottom of the sea was carried to the tip of the rhythmically shifting needle. The needle left delicate zigzag strokes on the paper. As long as the zigzag lines retained their uniform regularity, no untoward tremors were occurring deep beneath the earth or on the mountain.

Jinpei recalled the words of Kinoshita's answer when he had telephoned from the hospital not so long ago. Casually Jinpei took the smoked paper in his hands and let his eyes run over it. Then all of a sudden he observed his hands tremble ever so little.

In three distinct places near one end of the trailing smoked paper the zigzag recording showed unusual variations.

'The machine needs readjusting.'

But the seismograph was not out of order, and neither had Jinpei misread the record, and he knew it. Akadaké was not supposed to betray him, yet there on the smoked paper were clearly revealed the ominous tremors suggesting an imminent explosion.

At that moment what crossed his brain was not the image of Akadaké as he had just observed it bathed in the hazy sunlight. What came to mind, and he didn't know why, was the face of his daughter-in-law Sakiko when all of a sudden at table this morning she had looked at him in derision. It flashed through his mind for only a moment, the phantom of that caustic smirk on her face.

The basement room was quiet; only the seismograph motor continued the rhythmical drone of its whirlabout motion. Jinpei, as though in collapse, sat down in a chair near the seismograph. For a while he listened again to the dull beats from the mechanism.

Perhaps Kato had returned. Jinpei heard a familiar raucous voice from the corridor.

'Suda San is here, they say. Where did he go?'

But Jinpei made no move to rise from the chair. He felt the voice of Kato coming to him from another world.

*   *   *

Laying his hand on the cement wall for support, Jinpei Suda mounted the stairs, a step at a time. He felt internal noises banging against his temples, the same symptoms that had plagued him on the night he had been invited to the Eiraku Inn.

'I'm going to faint again . . .'

Suddenly the noises banging at his temples turned to shrieks of laughter coming from a vast throng. The waves of laughter moved in a whirlpool that submerged him up to his ears, and then the waves subsided.

Jinpei stopped and closed his eyes for a while. When the laughing voices finally ceased, he was able to complete the climb. The brilliant sunlight flooding the corridor stung his eyes.

'Well, is that you, Chief? What a surprise!'

He heard the voice of Kato calling to him down the corridor. 'If I knew you were coming over, I would have stayed in the office, but . . .'

'Who's this?' muttered Jinpei, batting his eyes. With effort he made out the half-pint figure of the woman at Kato's side. Then he observed that she was a backland farm girl all dolled up for New Year's.

'This is my fiancée.'

Rather awkwardly, his former underling introduced the girl with her pinched homely face.

'I hope you will always be happy, Kato Kun.'

Again he heard the laughing voices beating at his inner ear. But he resisted, and made a mighty effort at saying something pleasant. Yet as he spoke, he felt the image of the young couple standing before his eyes gradually work a change to the image of another couple, his son and his daughter-in-law. And then there returned again the talk he had overheard from the hallway the night before. It came with a pain that tore the flesh of his heart.

'Is something troubling you?'

'No, no. Nothing at all.'

'I'll toast some *mochi* or something in the dining-room. Please join us in a bite to eat.'

'Well, thanks, but no young couple wants an old fellow like me hanging about. Three's a crowd. I'll be on my way.'

Kato tried to detain him, but Jinpei Suda pushed him aside and left through the main entrance. The sun was a bit hazy, but the sky was clear by now. In the quadrangle the same boys were shouting and throwing the ball as they had been. The noises banging within his skull came on again. Jinpei stopped in his tracks. He thought of how he had mentioned to Kato not a word about the erratic movements of the needle against the smoked paper. That's not all. He had taken the paper with him and now he had it tucked away in his pocket. He didn't have to remove the paper from his pocket. Those sinister zigzags marking the tremors were branded in his brain. They demonstrated that from last night until early this morning the underpinning of Akadaké had repeated its ominous quivering several times.

'Akadaké never plays me false.'

He mumbled the words beneath his breath, like an incantation. But Jinpei knew well that the words were losing their hypnotic power, losing even their meaning.

Suddenly that tremendous vortex of laughing voices came ringing back in his inner ear. 'Akadaké never plays you false?' The laughing voices came on louder, shriller. 'Not only Akadaké . . . You, you are disowned by all. You are disowned. You are disowned.' Deep in the laughing voices Jinpei felt that he could discern the derisive smirk on the face of Sakiko. Again he thought of the brutal talk of his son and his daughter-in-law that he had overheard from the hallway.

'Everybody hates him, but he keeps on living. Crap! the old bastard will be coming back . . .'

What had gone wrong? He was entirely conventional in his social life. He had never raised any waves. Certainly at home he was not a bad husband, not a bad father. Nevertheless, he was now forced to recognize the fact that he had never loved any one, and no one had ever loved him. Jinpei drew the smoked paper from his pocket. He tore it in two. Tearing the paper was futile, but Jinpei grasped at anything to relieve the pain within.

At a tobacco stand he caught sight of, he picked up the red pay telephone. The dull-witted voice of his wife came faintly over the wire.

'Hello . . . ,' Jinpei mumbled feebly.

'Hello . . . ,' came the weary response.

Behind his wife's voice he could hear a New Year's song. She had the radio playing. He pictured the scene – his wife had been taking a noonday nap, lying with her feet under the quilt that covered the *kotatsu*. He despaired of being able to make this woman understand the dryness of his soul, the anxiety of his loneliness.

'Listen . . . I am going . . .' Jinpei hesitated in silence. 'I won't be home until tonight.'

'Going where did you say?'

'Some business . . .'

Nothing more. He laid the phone on its cradle. He stood there for some time, making no effort to move along.

Naturally on New Year's Day, biggest holiday of the year, the harbour district was deserted. The sun was shining brightly down on Pier No. 2, which on business days, strong with the salty smell of the sea, was congested with workmen in rubber raincoats, and with the lorries to transport fish to the city. Today the sliding doors to the warehouses were hung with Shinto festoons. The doors were all locked tight. Only a handful of passengers were on the boat, ready for its run to the island. Tiny ripples made tiny sounds as they lapped against the prow. The bay was calm, and Akadaké looked hazy in the distance, bathed in the golden sunlight of New Year's Day.

'I worry too much. I'm getting old and I worry too much.'

Jinpei sat on a bench in the cabin and closed his eyes. This matter of closing his eyes – Jinpei tried to recall from his past how, as long as he managed to close his eyes on what was going wrong, in some way or other every problem solved itself. Come to think of it, such had been his way of life, his secret of survival.

In the third class cabin with him were a rowdy group of young fellows from the island, now heading home from their round of New Year's visits, loud-mouthed and loaded with *sake*. There were very few passengers, and yet the scratchy record blasted relentlessly into the cabin. The jet black hair on the young men's heads glistened with brilliant pomade. Their scarfs dangled sloppily out of their overcoats. They struck up a chorus geared to

the phonograph record. Jinpei stood up and headed for the open
deck as the boat swung about to start for the island.

Just outside the cabin door a foreigner in an old black overcoat
leaned against the wall. He was busy blowing his nose with a
dirty handkerchief. Then he wiped his eyes. Jinpei was flabbergasted to see the foreigner from the room next to his at the
hospital.

'Well, what a surprise!' He stopped short, then raised an
obsequious smile to his face. 'Are you going sightseeing on
Akadaké? My name is Suda. I'm in the room next to yours at
the hospital.'

The fellow-passenger said nothing, though he looked Jinpei
straight in the face.

'This boat here. I've taken the trip any number of times, you
know. Until this year I was head man in the Surveillance Section
at the Weather Bureau.'

The fellow-passenger stopped plying his handkerchief and
mumbled something or other, a switch that Jinpei interpreted
to mean that the man was warming to his company.

'I have a passionate interest in one thing only, Akadaké. Even
if I'm slowed up now with poor health, I can't pass up a visit to
the mountain.'

Because a certain look of curiosity began to light the eyes of
Durand, Jinpei forgot his mood of depression. He was now
starting on a high.

'If I have to say it myself, it's a funny thing, but . . . the
younger fellows at the Observatory always kidded me by calling
me "the Demon". And I'm still the Demon in spite of my age.'

'You're a demon, are you?' Durand smiled his irony.

'That's right. You see, in Japanese a man with a passionate
enthusiasm is often called a "demon".'

'What do you think, Suda San?' Durand edged close to Jinpei.
He took the considerable liberty of laying his hand on the shoulder of a Japanese acquaintance. 'In your opinion, this volcano
will never have another bad eruption, will it?'

'Any layman can figure that one out.' Jinpei shook his head
decisively in denial. 'Akadaké has grown old.'

'Just like you and me, eh?'

'Yes.'

Jinpei pulled himself away. He pointed toward the black bed of lava at the edge of the sea. The ship was slowly drawing closer to it.

'That's the deposit from back in the Era of Bunmei. There will never again be an eruption to match that one. Suppose there is another blow up – it will be like that recent explosion, throwing up maybe a handful of ashes.'

Durand began to click his tongue in disagreement. Nevertheless, Jinpei Suda launched into his monologue, word for word the same account of Akadaké's character which he had propounded for any number of people – how the centres of eruption had originated from the mountain base, how gradually the centres had moved up to higher reaches of the mountain. It made no difference to him now whether Durand accepted the explanation or not. Either way, nothing could stop his torrent of speech. It was plain logorrhoea, an unconscious mechanism to dispel the dark cloud of uncertainty within him. Jinpei was out to convince his own uneasy heart. He prattled on and on, to squelch the ominous zigzags in the seismogram, the noises banging in his head, the terror of death, the ghastly chorus of laughing voices.

The boat began to swing around from south to east, preparing to enter the harbour at Shirahama. The wind whipped into flapping tattoos the canvas covers of the lifeboats perched on deck.

Durand kept a contemptuous eye on the profile of Suda's face. He wore the same thin smile.

'To put it briefly, Suda San, everything you say about Akadaké is nothing more than what was discovered by Dr Koriyama from Kyoto U. But I'm a foreigner, and if you'll let me say something . . .'

Durand waved his big hand to keep Jinpei from speaking further.

'Your defence of Akadaké is true to form for the Japanese, who consider nature itself to be a god.'

Suda failed to grasp the patronizing tone of the foreigner's words.

'What do you mean?'

Durand broke out in a hoarse laugh. Then he wiped his face
with the handkerchief, and without another glance at Jinpei he
hobbled away on his cane towards the other end of the deck.

On the bus that runs up the mountain out of Shirahama, Durand
and Suda occupied seats some distance from each other. This
time it was Jinpei who was trying to avoid further contact with
this bumptious foreigner. Nevertheless, when the bus began to
gasp for breath on a steeper grade in the pumice-stone road,
Jinpei stole a look at his adversary, who was himself wearing
the usual suggestion of a smile as part of his unflinching scrutiny
of Jinpei.

Arriving at Point Shimoné on the Third Station level, the
foreigner headed for the door without even a civil sign towards
Jinpei, while the Japanese gentleman in turn waited for the
threadbare overcoat and the cane to disappear from the bus
before he made his unobtrusive exit. The sky was clearer today
than it had been that time he came with Aiba and Sasaki. Durand
was treading the pumice-stone road with considerable difficulty.
Jinpei deliberately took a different tack, descending a path going
down the slope on his right.

Through a filigree of trees Akadaké exposed to him the entire
expanse of her body. She seemed so close that a man might
touch her if only he put out his hand. Around the Fifth Station
level, and at the Sixth, her skin was powdered with grey volcanic ash, while here and there appeared the blemish of scattered boulders and yellowish festers of shrub growth. Today the
naked eye picked out details that normally called for binoculars.

A little bird twittered a song and then flew off. All was hushed.

Jinpei kept his eyes carefully glued to the ground, watching
for the dead remains of spiders or any of the charred birds.
Happily he found nothing of the kind. The sweet pure air came
up in a breeze through the wooded ravine on his left. As Aiba
had laughingly remarked on that other occasion, there wasn't
trace enough of hydrogen sulphide for a single stinker of a fart.

'The mountain is safe as ever . . . Why was I so worried?'

Then he recalled the time he had spoken half-jokingly to his
underlings at the observatory: 'When my turn comes to die,

please arrange for me a "burial-at-mountain" up on Akadaké.'

If there was a vocable in the language for 'burial-at-sea', it was just as easy to coin another for 'burial-at-mountain',* The nonce-word came to him again, firing his imagination, compelling his emotion. He had never given serious thought to dying, but enveloped now in the mountain silence, he felt it would be a natural thing were he to die at this moment. As he had grown old, so Akadaké had grown old; were he to die now, he could lie forever on the mountain, earth to earth, dust to dust, ashes to ashes. The thought was profoundly consoling to Jinpei – no more fear of death, no more suffering from the likes of Ichiro and Sakiko and Taka, no more striving for success, no more slaving only to live. Death, he thought, opened the door to eternal repose on the bosom of Akadaké.

He was startled by a muffled sound from underfoot. Some baby rabbit had perhaps disturbed a pebble. The noise from the pebble emphasized the utter stillness of the scene.

'Grown old along with Akadaké . . .

A second time he caught the muffled sound as of another pebble falling, like an echo from the deep bottom of a well.

Hesitantly Jinpei gazed into the ravine. He took note for the first time of a peculiarity on the north wall. He saw reddish-brown soil exposed, a scar of erosion stretched like a belt along the steep embankment.

Gravel and small stones were dropping from there to the bottom of the deep ravine.

There was no more room for doubt. A man with any knowledge about volcanoes would recognize the reddish-brown soil and the erosion as unmistakable warning signs of imminent danger. The subterranean volcanic heat, demanding clearance for explosive release, was searching out the softest spot on the surface. The ground is like a toasting *mochi* suspended over burning coals. The cake of *mochi* gradually expands with inner heat until the skin cracks open. So an eroding crack in the surface of a volcano foretells a new eruption.

Laying both hands to his temples, Jinpei shook his head. He

* *Suiso* = 'burial-at-sea'; *sanso*, the nonce-word = 'burial-at-mountain'.

tried not to hear the sound of the pebbles, but the dull echo of the stones falling to the bottom of the gully worked its way through the space between his fingers. And not only the sound of the stones . . .

Those loud guffaws, the jerky laughing as from a vast multitude, came ringing to his inner ear.

A gentle breeze from the escarpment on his left helped to cool Durand's perspiring face, but his weak heart found it difficult to navigate the uphill road of pumice stone. After some fifty yards, he was forced to stop, leaning on his cane, waiting for his dizzy feeling to right itself.

'Why did I come this far?'

The word 'obsession' was flittering in his brain, because St Theresa's Villa had preoccupied his mind for months. His sole desire was for a blast to come some day from the volcano, for the smoke and lava flow to overwhelm this house of God and flush it off the face of the earth.

About half-way up the hill Durand's shoulders were heaving for lack of breath. He stopped to wipe his face with the handkerchief. Feeling better, he put a cigarette between his lips but his hands were shaking far too much to get it lighted.

Four or five coolies were clearing out some brushwood. A man wearing knickers walked slowly up the hill in his direction.

'Are they going to build Theresa Villa here?'

Durand called to him as pleasantly as he could manage, but the man's rugged features clouded over with suspicion.

'I don't know, this is the site for a hotel.'

The man kept his sharp look fixed on Durand's receding figure. Any feeling of nausea is bad for a weak heart. As he progressed, Durand had for some time been hawking his slobber on the ground, and after all the spitting the inside of his mouth felt dry as desert dust.

'Hey, is it Durand?' He heard a voice call from up above.

On the brink of the low escarpment to his left stood the figure of Father Sato, his hands hidden inside his cassock. There was a student with him.

'Good to see you! But why up here?'

'I came to see Theresa Villa, Sato San.' As usual he put an insolent laugh in his voice, but the laugh broke down, he was so short of breath. 'You see, I too have an interest in the villa, a very personal interest.'

Father Sato gazed at the ruined former priest with pity and sympathy. 'It's not built yet. So far we've only been able to clear the land. There isn't much to see, but do have a look.'

'How big is the property?'

'A thousand *tsubo*, because the land is so cheap . . . You should have waited another month before coming.'

'It'll all be finished a month from now?'

'No, only the chapel. But when the chapel is ready, I'll be having the Christians here in a group.'

Father Sato was disconcerted by the cynical look on Durand's face. He spoke to the student beside him, saying, 'You'll join us then, won't you?'

The student remained silent.

'Give it a try, living in the pleasant surroundings of nature. It's the way to get rid of useless anxieties . . .'

As Father Sato had said, they had only started clearing the land. Under a sky now beginning to cloud over, the extensive site lay bared of any trees. The harvest of brushwood, with leaves still intact, was piled up here and there. Nothing had yet been done to excavate the reddish-brown lava rock exposed on the surface.

A flight of five or six birds cut across the sky in formation.

'It's three months now, Durand San. At first the plan was 400 *tsubo*. But with the Bishop's help, to my surprise I was able to acquire a thousand *tsubo*.'

Father Sato wasted no time in his approach to Durand. He raised his arm and sawed the air to describe the house of retreats soon to be built on the tilted site.

'It's a pity I didn't bring the blueprints, but in general I'll put the meeting hall over there, and the chapel will be next to it. On this side will be the overnight sleeping quarters and the dining-room.'

Durand reconstructed in his imagination the architectural

drawings he had seen on the wall in the rectory on Christmas Eve.

'Really, Durand San, it has been my long-standing dream. You know, even one week out of the year would be great. I want to be with the parishioners, get away from the wickedness of the world, lead a life of prayer and meditation. That's my ambition.'

It was too much to expect the pudgy Japanese pastor to detect the angry jaundiced feelings seething in Durand, so gloriously intoxicated was he in his own heaven-kissing euphoria.

'We can live like in a monastery. We'll have a regular order of the day, focused on the triad of daily Mass, private prayer, and labour. That's my plan.'

'If one is a Christian, Sato San, can anybody come?' Durand put his question with a straight face, as though he were profoundly impressed with Sato's explanation.

'Of course, of course. Even non-Christians, provided they are well disposed for seeking the way of truth . . .'

'How about a person who has given up the faith, like me?'

This time Father Sato caught the scent of Durand's mischief. In his naïveté his eyes began to blink and his face went red.

'Sato San . . . I'm only joking,' guffawed Durand. 'I have no desire to be taught another lesson on how to keep my place, the way the people did at Christmas only a week ago.'

He said no more, but turned to study the thousand *tsubo* of land spread out before his eyes. Looking directly across the plot he saw the south-east prominence of Akadaké. The slender column of thin smoke was rising from the top. The volcano will explode no more? So believed the pudgy Japanese priest standing near him. So believed the old man named Suda, whom he'd talked to on the boat today while coming to the island.

Be that as it may, the mountain would have to explode. If this volcano were nothing more than some aged thing in ugly grey-skinned wrinkles, would it not be out of proportion to the painful oversupply of evil in the world of humankind? Moral evil was not a thing to grow old and weak and die off like a mountain. In the mind of Durand Akadaké had ceased to be merely a natural phenomenon, merely another mountain. For months on end he had wiped his nose and mopped his tears by the hospital window while he studied Akadaké. He had come to realize that Akadaké had a personality of its own, like himself, like any human being. Once one grants that evil never departs from a man, then one was compelled to expect that the abdominal rumbles and the power to vomit black lava would never depart from Akadaké. In his imagination Durand had painted a picture of the day when a red pillar of fire would suddenly burst from a spot on the mountainside, when the deluge of lava hidden in yellow smoke would roll with dull reverberations through the present site, when the chapel of St Theresa's Villa would be buried in the torrent of evil, when the assembly hall would be cooked to a crisp in the flames.

'Sato San . . . we'll say no more.'

Durand broke out in another half-maniacal laugh. At that, the student who had been with Father Sato rejoined them. He stole a curious look, first at the flabbergasted priest, then at the foreigner.

Durand was expecting some kind of charitable hand-out, and true to his expectation, on the boat returning to the city Father Ginzo Sato approached him unobtrusively.

'Here . . . I haven't much on me today, but please accept this little.'

Without further ado he pressed some paper money into his hand, while Durand with a curl on his lip slid the money into the pocket of his ragged overcoat. As always with these private doles from Father Sato, Durand felt again the painful pleasure of his own degradation.

Night had settled on the city. The bloodless fluorescent street lights were aglow – a recent civic improvement in the dockside district. But the streets in contrast were deserted, eerily quiet, because it was New Year's Night. The church lay in an opposite direction from the hospital, so the priest bade farewell to Durand.

'I'll see you at the hospital, sometime,' he said.

But Durand was quite aware that the kindly priest wanted in fact to drop the connection with him. He had insight enough to

understand that were it not for the prick of a conscience rooted
in a sense of moral superiority and a sense of duty, the priest
would never again set foot in the hospital.

The fog of the night had begun to enfold the low-slung Japanese houses. Every dwelling burned a dim light bulb in a small
room where the family was eating supper. Durand always
thought, from when he first came to this land, that the streets
never seemed so deserted and dingy as on the night of New
Year's Day. A single empty tram car ran close to him and loped
away. An open sewer flowed parallel to the tracks. The sewer
hit him in the nose. A lone white rubber shoe was floating on
the slops.

The street was straight, and he became aware of the student
following him but being careful to maintain his distance – the
student who had accompanied him and Father Sato. Durand
decided to stop, with a pretence of inspecting the sewer. The
student stopped short. Durand saw that even a young man like
this one was chary of him. He wondered if he appeared to the
student like something contaminated. Again he felt inside that
mixture of pain and morbid pleasure.

'You must be tired, my boy . . . are you not?' Durand called
to him while he went through the motions of taking a standing
pee at a protected corner on the street. 'I'm heading for the
hospital. Where are you going?'

The student answered quietly that he had a room in the
neighbourhood of Shinmei-cho.

'You've been a Christian from way back, have you?' Durand
brazenly laid his hand on the student's shoulder and whispered,
'In the days when I myself was a priest the students were
always my favourite.'

Under his hand he felt the student's skinny shoulder quiver.
Durand was swept by a sudden impulse – to experiment at
seducing this young man.

'But I quit the priesthood, you know. I lost all interest in
doing church work here in Japan, the way that Sato San carries
on.'

The student looked up at him bewildered.

'Here's the reason. You seem different from the usual

simple-minded Christian, so you'll appreciate the point, I think. I know for a fact that the Japanese people in general cannot believe in God. Because the Japanese don't need any God . . . You yourself, tell me the truth, you don't really believe in God.'

Under his hand the skinny shoulder trembled more than ever. But Durand felt in the animal heat of the lad that the pleasure of the tempter was beginning to melt together with the pleasure of the one being tempted. He felt the student dissolving in doubt.

'You go to church regularly. But still, you don't really believe it. Yes, I know about that. You do bad things. But you're not particularly sorry. You're not sorry at all. Isn't that the way it is?'

In the dusky haze of the night the foreigner and the Japanese student stood stock still, facing each other. A man drove by on a bicycle. He threw a glance at Durand and the student, then pumped his bike towards the main street.

'I'll teach you something nice.'

Durand drew his face close to the face of the student.

'If a man doesn't feel guilty of any sin, he doesn't have to depend on God. You Japanese don't have any feelings of guilt, do you?'

He reached his hand into his coat pocket where his fingers touched the two thousand yen in paper money which Father Sato had given him today. It could be fun to use the money on something that the pudgy priest himself would never suspect. Durand slipped the money into the student's palm and closed his hand around it.

'This is a New Year's gift. In Japanese language you call it "o-toshidama". Take this money and for once in your life – well, go and do something, even something bad. It'll be fun to test yourself, to see if your conscience hurts, after doing something dishonourable.'

Then without a glance back at the student, Durand turned and started down the street on his cane. Another tram car overtook him and ran on past. His day's activity came to an end, enough for *that* day.

'Sacré vieux chien . . . sacré vieux chien.'

EIGHT

One day is like another in the hush of senile weakness.

The second day of *Shogatsu* was another dull time for Jinpei in his own home. He had three days' hospital leave to celebrate the new year, but on the second day there was nothing to do, nowhere to go. He spent the whole time in the living-room with both hands tucked beneath the heavy quilt overlying the *kotatsu*. He sat there staring witlessly at the garden, withered now in winter's grip.

Every year there had always been a few people calling to pay respects to the Surveillance Section Head, even on New Year's Day itself. Young fellows from the office, like Kato and Suzuki, would come to see him, though they might be flushed and drunk on *toso* before they got around to Jinpei's house. But this year nobody came, not even on the second day. Were people scared away by his illness? Perhaps, but more likely they had crossed the old man off their list for being of no further use to them in life.

No doubt about it. Jinpei Suda was nothing but a thing whose very existence need no longer be recognized. He stayed put, seated in the *kotatsu*, ruminating on his true condition for the first time, occasionally mumbling something to himself.

In the barren wintry garden a line of flower pots was standing on a shelf. The potted plants had never been of any great value, being odds and ends brought home for example from a walk to the festival at some shrine or other in the company of his younger son. Beyond his love for coming to grips with Akadaké, Jinpei had no other hobby worthy of the name. Still, he did enjoy applying the trimming shears. That was before he became ill.

Now the plants were totally neglected. Some had died, and

even the survivors were covered with dust. The layer of dirt
was not the only sign of the garden's total neglect, for on the
little pond in the centre floated an old rubber shoe.

Were it still the good old days, he would now be calling to
Taka and scolding her for this or that, but today he had no
complaints. His vacant stare remained immovably fixed on a
single spot in the garden.

'Dad, shall I toast a cake of *mochi* for you?'

His wife spoke to him. It was three in the afternoon. Jinpei
failed to respond, but Taka laid a grill on top of the *hibachi* and
arranged some *mochi* on it. When the cakes were browned to
a turn, she painted them with soy sauce creating a delicious
aroma. Taka looked at him sitting there and staring listlessly
into the garden. He did extend a hand to accept the *mochi* cake,
but he didn't eat it. She began to feel concern.

'Aren't you feeling well?'

There was no reply.

'What seems to be the trouble?'

'Nothing.'

He did use his tongue, and Taka felt relief. She got to her
feet. She had the kitchen duties again today, Sakiko having gone
to visit her own family.

Evening came. Twilight enfolded the garden and stole across
the verandah into the living-room. The dusky room grew chilly
by degrees. Jinpei, however, made no move to pull his legs
from the *kotatsu*. He just stared at the gathering dusk as though
it were the winged shadow of some ominous bird. Taka brought
a hand shovel loaded with charcoal into the room. Had she
looked closely she might have perceived that her husband now
and then was moving his lips ever so faintly, as though speaking
to himself. But still he kept his rigid position, completely ignor-
ing his wife's presence.

From time to time the raucous voices of the many-headed
crowd continued ringing in his ear, whirling in a vortex then
ebbing away – the same laughing voices he heard on the mountain yesterday. Closing his eyes he saw again in his imagination
the reddish-brown scar along the canyon wall. And then at times
he heard the rocky fragments rolling down the side, like stones

falling deep to the bottom of a well from where they echoed back.

But today the echo of the stones conveyed no terror, nor even surprise. He felt, too, that the reddish-brown colour was only natural, natural yet unrelated to him, for the colour came to him as from some other unrelated world. So the whole day long he stared at the garden in its winter sleep, listening to the voices, hearing nothing but the voices.

The following day was already the third of *Shogatsu*, the day on which Jinpei was under doctor's orders to return to the hospital. Again he kept himself tucked inside the *kotatsu*, as he had done the day before. Now and then his lips would move as he muttered to himself.

The weather carried a threat of snow. Sometimes his younger son, the junior high school boy, disturbed his quiet by racing noisily along the verandah. He never objected. Sakiko, coming home from the visit to her family, showed her face in the living-room. Standing at the threshold, removing the woollen scarf worn as a cover on her head, she favoured him with no more than the suggestion of a conversation.

'Hi, I'm back. And Aiba San is here too.'

Noting his empty-eyed expression, she raised on her face the usual thin smile, cold and contemptuous.

Jinpei took hold of his tea mug and managed a weak nod of comprehension. Then the city councilman barged into the house, speaking boisterously at Taka.

'It's strange weather, Mrs Suda. It's beginning to snow.'

Sure enough, tiny white flakes were visible blowing gently about the garden. The mild climate of the city normally called for only a single snowfall in a year. Aiba reminded Taka that since the end of the war this was only the second time they'd had a white *Shogatsu*.

'We should be paying our respects with a New Year's call at *your* house,' Taka said. 'But my husband being so poorly . . .'

'Don't talk like that, Mrs Suda.' The councilman slid his legs down into the *kotatsu*. From his sitting position he removed his Inverness cape.

'Suda Kun, we're finally ready to start building. We have finished clearing the site and grading it. And thanks to you, our friend Sasaki is all excited about the prospects, even more than I am.'

His manner of speech showed how he had forgotten all about the time he had come flying to the hospital with the scientific journal.

'I had you doing a lot of the leg work, and I . . .'

But the eyes of Jinpei from behind his glasses beheld the relentless waggle of Aiba's mouth without reaction. His leaden eyes indicated that he wasn't even listening to the other's gabble. But the imperceptive city councilman began to unwrap the kerchiefed bundle which he had brought, exposing a gift box of fancy cookies, saying to Taka, who at that moment appeared with tea, 'Mrs Suda, this is nothing, just a token . . .'

A folded set of building plans fell to the floor from under the gift box. Aiba spread the blueprints on top of the *kotatsu*, wetting his fingers several times to manipulate the printed sheets while he explained.

'The plans are drawn according to my own design. I had them done in the latest American style. Our tourist industry can no longer attract foreign visitors with the type of service found in Japanese-style inns. That's the reason.'

Dazedly Jinpei recalled the scene at Akadaké as he had seen it from Point Shimoné after the bus ride on the day before yesterday. He saw in his imagination the cover of grey volcanic ash at the Fifth Station and at the Sixth. He saw the great masses of rock protruding here and there on the mountain surface, the details as clear as they had been when viewed before with field glasses.

Snow was visible through the windows, falling harder now. The cover of dust on the potted plants was faintly overlaid in white. Jinpei had the illusion of looking through the swirling snow to see the canyon wall and the reddish-brown band of erosion stretched along it.

'Suda Kun. What's the matter? Your face looks pale.'

Jinpei weakly wagged his head. Aiba shook the ash of his cigar into his tea cup before he said, 'Incidentally, the business of publishing your book. Your manuscript isn't ready yet, I don't suppose?'

Suda didn't reply.

'How is it progressing, Suda Kun?'

'Nothing,' said Jinpei Suda in a weary voice. 'Because I decided . . . to wait a while.'

'How's that?'

Since the councilman got no more reaction than some barely detectable mumbling movement of the lips, he dropped the subject and turned his attention back to the blueprints. His hefty frame and fat neck were throbbing with an enthusiasm totally immune to the troubles tormenting Jinpei.

'The stones slide down . . . ,' Jinpei mumbled scarcely audibly.

'Stones? . . . What do they do?'

'The sound of the stones . . . I can hear them.'

Aiba looked up in surprise at the painful vertical creases formed on the old man's brow. Jinpei cradled his head in both his hands.

'Where do you hear it? I can't hear any stones anywhere.'

Still holding his hands to the sides of his head, Jinpei Suda turned a woebegone face to Aiba.

'Don't do that! Suda San!'

The city councilman was distressed. He got to his feet, utterly flustered.

'Don't do that. *Mrs Suda*! Where are you?'

Jinpei waved a hand to control Aiba's shouting. Taka, hearing the clamour, ran from the kitchen into the living-room. Aiba, with one hand supporting the sick man's head, slowly lowered Jinpei back onto the *tatami*.

Jinpei's eyes were open wide. He offered no resistance. He lay flat on his back, his eyes staring up, his feet still dangling inside the *kotatsu*.

'We have to call a doctor. You do it, Mrs Suda.'

'Call the doctor? I'll be all right in a minute.' The stubborn old man rolled his head from side to side in refusal. 'It's a slight relapse. Just let me lie here quietly.'

Sakiko and Jiro too, having heard the commotion, ran into the living-room. Jinpei was now besieged by the whole family, while he continued to stare at the ceiling. Yet amazingly, when anybody spoke to him, he found the strength to answer. So the family decided to wait a while before summoning the doctor.

'Is that a fact? . . . You say Suda San went up Akadaké on New Year's Day? Nobody mentioned it to me, I had no idea.'

Aiba expressed genuine surprise when he heard the story from Taka.

'It's probably exhaustion from that. Who could have supposed . . . going up again on Akadaké . . .'

When the family once more turned its attention to Jinpei, his head had rolled to one side and he breathed with a light gurgling sound. From his open mouth the saliva was running down his chin, forming a little puddle on the *tatami*. Two months before, the first time he was stricken, the same thing had happened.

Jinpei stood on the rim of the canyon at the Third Station level He was looking down the valley, intently studying the surface, but nowhere could he discover the reddish-brown soil exposed. The stunted pine brush and the clumps of trees completely covered the left-side slope. Behind him stood Councilman Aiba and Sasaki peering into the canyon with similar apprehensive looks.

Then Aiba said with satisfaction, 'I don't see the signs of erosion in the canyon wall. With construction of the hotel progressing as it is, we can't have an eruption or anything like that.'

Above the canyon rim rose the bare ribbed framework of the three-storey structure already in place. A swarm of coolie workmen were visible crawling along the framework.

'You permitted us to advance this far with the building Suda San. If an explosion or anything does occur, the responsibility falls on you.'

Jinpei assented with a nod that was more like a flinch of fear. To be sure, as the councilman said himself, no odour of gas was lingering in the vicinity, and the reddish-brown scar of erosion had vanished from the canyon wall. 'And yet I really saw the scar . . . with my own eyes I saw it.' Somewhere in his brain lurked something that frustrated his attempts to drive away his fear. Nevertheless, the dull echoes from falling rocks were no longer to be heard. The valley was serenity itself. A single tiny bird chirped its song and flew away.

The sky began to cloud. Slowly the dark shadow of the haze rolled its way as low as the middle reaches of Akadaké. It seemed too that a wind was beginning to blow. When he noticed it, the figures of Aiba and Sasaki had vanished, and in their place behind him stood a stern-faced Dr Koriyama.

'Professor! Akadaké proved to be an old worn out volcano after all. But it caused me lots of worry.' Jinpei produced a fawning smile. 'Your theory was absolutely right.'

'Suda Kun. With volcanoes, don't speak of worn out ones nor dormant ones.' His answer was unaccountably surly.

'You cannot reckon a volcano in terms of centuries. Without probing in terms of thousands of years, one cannot know.'

'Maybe so, but you yourself first proposed my theory, did you not?'

'I didn't know.'

'But you can't say, "I didn't know."'

Jinpei panicked. He grabbed the learned man's clothing, but the clothing slipped through his fingers as the professor gave him a cold-hearted glance, then departed, dragging a crippled leg, up towards the crater peak, where the wind blew.

When Jinpei turned around, the look of the valley had changed. Until a moment ago the canyon walls were covered by the thick-growing brush, but in a trice several reddish-brown bands of eroding surface had reappeared. He saw that everywhere along the crumbling strata huge black rocks were one by one coming loose and crashing into the ravine. When a rock struck one of the trees lower down on the steep slope, its course was diverted, and then with a final heavy thump it was swallowed into the lowest depths. When one rock had been gulped down, another rock on the reddish disintegrating surface would begin its slide. And that rock too, after it tumbled and disappeared, was followed in its fall by still another rock.

By and by numerous jets of steamlike smoke began to spurt from the reddish-brown soil. At first the smoke was a white and wispy vapour, but little by little it turned to muddy yellow, and the jets grew in size, until they shot up over the canyon rim. By degrees the heat in the earth and the earth's uncertain tremors began to penetrate Jinpei's shoes.

The vast chorus of maniacal laughter rang in concert with the quaking of the earth. The shrieks of laughter echoed from the canyon wall and from the peak rising on his right until they engulfed him from every side. The earth's tremors through his shoes increased in magnitude.

As he wheeled about he saw nothing but smoke. Where were the others in the smoke – Sasaki? Aiba? Dr Koriyama? He couldn't find them. Like the roar of a rushing train the rumble of the earth came up from the deep of the canyon and over the rim. At that moment directly before his eyes he beheld the blast of a pillar of fire.

The round-shouldered doctor on holiday duty used the help of a nurse when he plunged the hypo needle into Jinpei's strangely resistant left arm. The reddish cylinder of injection slowly drained from the syringe.

'It seems that he suffered some kind of shock,' the doctor said, batting his eyes as he questioned both Taka and Ichiro and Ichiro's wife, who were standing near the bed.

'What do you mean when you say "shock"?'

'During these three days . . . did anything happen that might have unduly upset a man that's sick?'

But the family were puzzled. They could say nothing.

When the doctor removed the injection needle, the patient's body jerked in a spasm. Blood oozed from the needle wound but the nurse quickly staunched it by slapping a patch of adhesive over the puncture.

The electric light in the sick-room was depressingly dim. Through the wall they could hear the foreigner strenuously blowing his nose. It was shortly after 8 pm. The doctor made some notes on the chart, handed the nurse the tray on which rested the syringe and a roll of cotton, and then departed. The three remaining in the room stood for a time in silence, watching Jinpei's face. Characteristic of low blood pressure, his complexion was pale as paper. The weak glow from the light bulb played grisly make-up tricks with the sick man's nostrils and his unshaven chin.

'Mum, didn't you see anything?'

'What do you mean?'

'Anything that might have disturbed Dad.'

'I don't know . . . Today, and yesterday too, he was very quiet at home.'

Then Ichiro thundered how awful it was for a sick man to try a thing like going to Akadaké, that the old man did it only because he always had his own way. Meanwhile Sakiko being Sakiko, moved away from the bed and leaned her forehead against the pitch black window. The hospital was absolutely quiet, except when they heard another blow from the nose next door.

'Sakiko, how about you, don't you know something?'

'Who, me?'

She turned towards them, and again for another instant that sardonic smirk appeared on Sakiko's face.

'What's to be done?' continued Ichiro. 'The sick bills will pile up again. Listen Mum. Don't look to us for any assistance if money gets to be a problem.'

Taka was gripping the iron of the bedstead. She spoke quietly of her worries. She had the retirement bonus, but it was no bigger than a tear from the eye of a sparrow. She said she had used almost all of it to pay the hospital prior to *Shogatsu*.

'The injections are expensive,' she said.

'He probably never took out any insurance . . . Mum, don't be giving me that hard look. With Dad in this condition, you will . . .'

While the mother and son fought it out, Sakiko leaned on the wall in unconcern, gazing down on the night-time city scene. The excursion boat, ablaze with lights, was cutting across the jet black surf towards the island on its last scheduled run of the day. Sakiko turned her gaze to the shadow figures thrown on the dingy wall by her husband and his mother. She thought how she would have to keep living forever in the hold of these two phantoms. She herself would grow into the likes of old Taka, and she herself would become the one to figure the pay-off from the insurance. In her husband's house the stench of a different old man would be lingering in every corner, as it did in the present sick-room. She felt how, before she would realize it, the smell of that other old man would infect her own body parts. The over-cautious, over-careful face of Jinpei, the birdlike beady eyes of Taka, and Ichiro the master product from the two of them – she hated the thought, she hated it. Her mouth was close to the window where she breathed her sighs on the cold glass.

Jinpei remained in a coma for days on end. Sometimes he opened his languid eyes in an empty stare at whoever was sitting by his side, be it Taka, or Ichiro, or the nurse's aide. Then he slid back into a coma.

He beheld himself and Dr Koriyama picking their way across the enormous bed of lava dating from the Era of Bunmei. On the ninth day of the tenth month in the Eighth Year of Bunmei, the molten rock had gushed from Arimura-kami. From the Sixth Station level they clearly saw the black lava that rolled like a swollen river down as far as the sea. Here and there some rusty reddish patches of mountain slope showed through, where the massive lava rocks lay jumbled one against another in the black meandering of the river. To this day there wasn't a single shrub capable of taking root where they were standing. The sky was heavily overcast, and a solitary crow appeared against the lowering clouds. The crow pursued them always, its baleful caw sometimes sounding close above them, sometimes far away. Jinpei had heard stories of people who came to the uninhabitable lava to commit suicide.

'What a mountain of heart-ache it is. A volcano resembles human life.' Dr Koriyama muttered it with feeling. 'In youth it gives rein to the passions, and burns with fire. It spurts out lava. But when it grows old, it assumes the burden of those past evil deeds. It turns deathly quiet as we now behold it.'

· Jinpei was silent. This kind of talk was not his gift. Men with a reputation for learning speak in elevated sentences. He was munching on a ball of rice, lost in reverie.

'Nevertheless, Suda Kun, a human being is not entirely like the volcano. You and I, when we grow old, will cast a backward glance upon our lives, becoming fully aware of our mistakes. Don't you see?'

Slowly raising his eyes towards the ashen sky, towards the melancholic cawing from the solitary crow, the professor continued to speak.

'But when we do become aware of our mistakes – herein lies the tragedy of age, does it not? – we no longer have the time left to us to live again for the better.'

Jinpei stood up. He was sucking the pit of the pickled prune, all that was left from his rice ball. He removed the pit from his mouth and threw it as far as he could. The pit landed on the far side of the ravine, then fell in a zigzag course from one jagged rock to another.

Ichiro asked his mother, 'When did he take out the insurance? Show me the policy sometime.'

'Your father always kept these matters to himself.'

'I suppose your own name appears as beneficiary. Mine won't be mentioned.'

NINE

Somebody knocked on the door. It wasn't a nurse, because a nurse after two or three taps would never wait for an answer before wrenching the doorknob.

'Who's there, who is it?'

Durand was seated in the old rattan chair, the blanket wrapped around his hips. He rose to his feet but still he got no answer. It was strange indeed for anyone to visit him at such an hour. For a moment he thought it might be Father Sato. Yet he had taken leave of the priest at the pier hardly three hours before.

Durand reached out for the cane that stood against the wall and dragged his feet to the door.

'Oh-h, it's you, is it?' he said.

Standing in the dimly lit corridor was the young man dressed in the student uniform with its military collar. Looking down at the timidly tense face, Durand managed a smile.

'The money – how did you spend it?'

'I didn't spend it.'

'You don't say! . . . Come in.'

The lad walked into the overpowering body odour that seasoned Durand's room. He kept his eyes averted while standing rigidly straight and close to the wall. Today again the wrinkled sheets, stained with sweat to a mild brown colour, drooped from the bed to the floor. The table was scattered with dirty dishes and chopsticks.

'Well then, what happened?'

The boy reached awkwardly into his pocket, then laid the neatly folded banknotes on the table. The action coaxed a smile from Durand in spite of himself. Not only a smile. The boy's act excited in him an impulse to besmirch the tense pallid face, like the excitement of deciding to smash some freshly picked fruit under muddy boots.

'So after all, you didn't use the two thousand yen. Well, young fellow, I'm not asking you to return it. Go and spend it on something, on anything you like.'

Durand swallowed hard, then broke off his talking, but only for a little.

'I won't know what you do. Nobody else will know.'

Far down the corridor somebody was astir with flapping slippers. The footsteps halted in front of the toilet. They heard the squeal of the swinging toilet door. The only night sounds ever heard in the hospital were from the toilet door and from the flappy slippers of a patient walking the corridor.

'Why do you act like this?' The student's voice was croaking.

'It's to do you some good, and me too. Young man . . .'

Seated again in the rattan chair, Durand kept tapping his cane against a place on the wall.

'Why not try using the money on something, without telling Father Sato. Without going to confession. Enjoying the secret all by yourself.'

'What's in it for you?'

'Well, it's because I want to find out.'

Durand kept fiddling with the cane even when he raised his eyes to steal a look at the student.

'Keeping a secret from Father Sato – I want to find out if you can do it without your conscience hurting. Understand?'

Durand could finally hear the student heaving his tortured heavy breaths. 'There! He's taken the bait. If I play the rod a little bit more, I'll hook him.'

'I don't think you'll have any problem. First of all, even I won't be seeing what you use the money for. You can throw it into the river for all I care, and . . .' He pulled out the dirty handkerchief and covered his nose and mouth. He watched the student intently with eyes unwontedly ablaze.

'You might go to a house and get a woman. Even for a thing like that, if you have a couple of thousand yen, wouldn't that be enough? Anyway, you can do it, with nobody being the wiser

. . . you can test your own self. Once is all you need to make
the test. To find out if you really believe, to find out if you have
a conscience that will bother you after a sin. Won't that be fun
to know?'

Durand stood up and moved slowly towards the table. The
paper money, folded in two, was flanked by two dirty dishes.
When his fingers closed on the money, the words of Father
Sato crossed his mind, the words softly whispered into Durand's
ear when they parted at the boat landing. Whispered not only
today, they were the words which the Japanese priest invariably
spoke each time he came to the hospital, each time he favoured
Durand with cigarettes or a basket of fruit.

'I myself don't mind your coming to the church, but it's the
problem of scandalizing the people. Please be understanding.'

That pharisaical way of being a virtuous man, that unctuous
manner of speech. The thought of it abruptly stirred the bile in
the soul of Durand.

'I'm giving you a present, my boy. It's strange that you don't
take it. The way I see it, I only want to give you a treat for
New Year's.'

Durand grabbed the student's rigid fingers. He could feel the
fingers tremble ever so little.

'Here . . . Nobody else knows. Nobody's watching what we
do.'

Then he opened the door and ushered the student out. When
he closed the door he bated his breath, waiting for sounds from
the other side. Durand could feel the boy standing motionless
in the darkened corridor. Then after a while he heard the steps
moving away on tip-toe. Durand leaned on the wall and wrinkled
his brow. He wiped his frown with the handkerchief. Again he
twisted his face, this time using force to create a smile.

In his delirium Jinpei was totally unaware of being carried back
to the hospital. The place that he saw in his dream was not the
house in which he had spent the days of *Shogatsu*. Indistinctly
it was like the house in the Kirishima District where he and
Taka had lived for nearly twenty years before his repatriation

to the local observatory. That house had been in Manchuria, in the city of Dairen.

He recognized the Dairen house from the soot-covered frozen snow that covered the garden and lay piled high on the roofs of the neighbours' houses visible beyond. The snow was black with gritty smoke from the *pechika* in every house. The furnishings inside the house were even more familiar – the sideboard holding the tea set, the pendulum clock hanging on one of the house posts, and on the wall a picture of Their Majesties, the Emperor and the Empress, arrayed in their coronation robes.

But it was dark in the house and cold. It was night and winter. A pale gleam from the frozen snow in the garden revealed the windows. It seemed to Jinpei that he himself had just returned from his work at the weather station.

He pulled the sliding partitions one by one to find that his house was deserted. He called his wife by name, without effect. She was not to be found in any of the rooms. His dirty tea bowl sat on the living-room table as he had left it, only half drained. He stuck his head in the kitchen and still he couldn't find her.

Now it came to him with a shock that his wife had deserted him. He couldn't prove it to himself, but somehow he knew that Taka was gone from their house forever. She never would return to him.

In Jinpei's scheme of things, Taka was never anything more than a helpmeet. He viewed the married state as being no more than a social convention, a practical arrangement in which the very essence of a wife lay in the menial service of washing his clothes, packing his lunch, looking after his child. In Jinpei's mind the number one consideration was always social decorum. Once he and Taka were married, he never touched another woman, not because he loved his wife, but rather because in a tight community like Dairen even the most circumspect affair would stir up a hornet's nest of gossip. A long time ago one of his colleagues had taken up with a woman from the Japanese restaurant in the city's Naniwa district. It wasn't long before the affair became common knowledge among his fellow workers. And no sooner did it reach the ear of higher authority than the man was demoted and forthwith removed to the Manchurian outpost of Fushun. Consequently, when it dawned on Jinpei in the darkened house that his wife had run away, the first reaction was not heartache for Taka, nor lurid suspicions, nor jealousy. It was consternation at the thought of her doing a thing so outrageous to him.

Jinpei knew he would become the butt of ridicule and snide remarks from colleagues and from the higher echelons, as soon as word got around that his wife had deserted him. The houses in either direction from his own in the row were designated official residences for Weather Service personnel. The term 'official residence' sounds good, but in reality the dwellings were nothing but flat-topped, single storeyed piles of brick, each containing three compartments, one of eight-*tatami* size, another of six, and still another of only four and a half. Casting a nervous eye at the dirty snow piled on the roofs of one house after another, Jinpei flinched at the thought that every house might be concealing a woman already aware of his wife's disappearance.

Then gradually anger took over. After twenty years of sweat he had finally attained the dignity of serving as stand-in for his Section Head at the weather station. This dignity was done with, all on account of his wife. 'I took good care of that woman for twenty years. I kept working for her and the baby,' he grumbled. 'What on earth did I do wrong?'

Hidden deep in his resentment was the chagrin at having lost an object of enormous convenience. He realized how tough his daily life was going to be in the absence of Taka. Now that he had lost her, he came to appreciate the practical value of that person whose very presence beside him he rarely acknowledged. From this day forward, he would have to do the laundry and the cooking himself. Another woman was unthinkable. To take in a second spouse, fit her into his routine, train her to his own life-style, was too much trouble for a man of his age.

He had absolutely no idea why his wife had disappeared. The house was cold and dark. In his dream, Jinpei began to wonder if the whole thing wasn't merely a dream. Without changing from his business suit, he sat down, crossing his legs and facing the living-room table. He picked up the tea bowl. He saw in the

bottom of the bowl the yellow dregs of the tea only half con-
sumed in his haste to leave the house that morning. Through
the kitchen doorway the cat peered into the living-room, moved
slowly in his direction, and snuggled into his lap. He kept strok-
ing the cat with one hand, but otherwise sat motionless, hypno-
tized now by watching the dusk falter into night against the
frozen snow in the garden.

There was a hardly perceptible sound from the direction of
the kitchen. Forcibly Jinpei brushed the cat from his lap and
raced to the spot. He found nothing but grime and burned out
matchsticks on the stove, the old iron pots and the kettle, the
shelf of dishes gleaming in the darkish gloom.

The vision abruptly shifted scene to a long, straight road
through the snow. Every year in Dairen, when winter came,
the coolies went to work with shovels pitching the snow to the
side of the street. Lined up on the sidewalk at intervals were
mountainous piles of the stuff.

Ichiro was still a baby, and his wife had him strapped to her
back. In his dream her face was amazingly the face of a Taka
still in the bloom of youth.

Jinpei walked silently beside her along the street with its piles
of snow. Now and then an ass-drawn cart drove past the couple,
barely avoiding them. 'Ah-h, in the early years of Showa the
wagons drawn by these "Chinese horses" were what we used
for the taxicabs of today.' The Manchurian drivers cracked their
whips, and their noise gradually faded away in the distance
where the melancholy glow of the wagon lanterns disappeared
in the great beyond of the grey-toned road.

No matter how far he walked with her, it was to no avail.
Taka explained that her decision to leave was irreversible. He
could hardly believe that such a resolute voice could come from
the woman who up till now had always been so nervously intent
to catch the reaction in her husband's face when she did get the
courage to disagree.

'Only tell me why, then I won't even try to hold you back.'
Failing in the effort to control his excitement, Jinpei began to
scream. 'But never forget that after you're gone, it won't bother
me in the least. That's all I've got to say.'

'I'm well aware of that,' said Taka quietly, 'because you're that kind of person.'

'If you think you're hurting me, you're making a bad mistake. You'll be the loser. Try giving some thought to your own best interests.'

He wasn't aware of having been unfaithful to his wife, as other men were, no not even once. He had never disturbed the good order of their home. For the moment he was even persuaded that he never touched his lips to *sake*, or even to a cigarette, except perhaps at some dinner party with his colleagues. In no sense of the word did he think that he was a bad husband. For twenty full years he had never ceased working to support his wife and the child. However much he might search his heart, there was no reason to expect that he would uncover the memory of any act that had drawn the least criticism from Taka or any one else. When one got down to facing facts, she herself would be the one to suffer if she walked out on such a family. With considerations of this kind Jinpei strained his rhetorical powers trying to change her mind.

At that moment Taka raised her head and looked him in the eye. Jinpei caught the faint sardonic sneer that crossed her face. (This smile he remembered having seen somewhere already. It was the smirking manner of his daughter-in-law Sakiko every time she looked at him.)

'I'll be the laughing stock of the world. Didn't you ever think about that? Everybody at the Weather Station will point their finger behind my back.'

'That's the whole trouble. The only thing that concerns you is that smug opinion of yourself. You . . . you never could love another person.'

Suddenly Ichiro began to cry. Taka tried to humour the baby strapped on her back, then she said to Jinpei quietly, 'That's all . . .'

'But there's more. What is it? If you could say that I was ever unfaithful to you . . .'

'I don't know, but it might have been better if you really had been unfaithful once in a while.'

Leaving behind that strange remark, his wife started walking in longer strides. The rubber boots worn over her pantaloons creaked on contact with the packed down snow.

'No! Please don't follow me.'

Jinpei stopped short and watched her move away. He still entertained the expectation that his wife would soon return. What she was doing was only a threat. He imagined that when she got to the end of the road, she would give some thought to her situation, to living expenses for herself, money to support the child. Then she would double back in her tracks.

Nevertheless, she maintained her gait, with the baby still on her back. She proceeded to the crest of the uphill road over which the wagons had disappeared. She never looked back. The sight of her dissolved in the haze of the night.

Again the dream shifted scenes. It wasn't Dairen any more. It was their present home. In the dead of night he was out in the hallway trying to get to the toilet. He couldn't locate the light switch. He directed his feet by feeling his way along the wall like a blind man. Just to the other side of his pitch dark world was the bedroom of Ichiro and Sakiko. He could catch their pillow talk leaking through the paper of the sliding panels.

'How about the doctor's fee and the hospital expenses?' It was the voice of Sakiko. 'Mother better not be asking us to cough it up.'

'The Old Man has probably spent all his retirement bonus, but crap! we really don't know. If he had only dropped dead right on the spot, the retirement bonus, the whole thing would have come to us intact. I don't like old people the way they are. They eat their rice off others, for free, and keep on living, a pain to everybody, and they never learn what a burden they are.'

'How does Mum feel about it?'

'The same as us, I really think so. When Dad collapsed, the one that felt relief was really Mum.'

The light in their room went off. The noise of a barking dog could be heard in the distance. A gloomy stillness enveloped the house.

Supporting his weight against the wall, Jinpei's eyes bulged out, staring into the dark. He had never recognized himself as being alienated, but this was the moment of truth when it came home to him how alone he had always been. In a lifetime of sixty years he had never expended whole-hearted love on a single human being, nor had he ever been loved in return by a single human being. For the first time in his sixty years of living he was face to face with the facts.

'When we have taken on the years, we look back on our past; and even though we come to know the mistakes we made, there is no time left to live again and repair the damage. The tragedy of old age, after all, lies precisely in this, does it not?'

Such were the words mumbled by Dr Koriyama sitting on the jet black lava. The words became like a taut wire to pinch off the heart of Jinpei, groping his way back to the bedroom where he sat on the floor bed beside his wife.

'What's bothering you?'

Jinpei thought that Taka was sleeping, but now he could feel that she too was lying there nervously tense with her own eyes bulging open to stare into the dark.

'I'll tell you . . .'

But his wife cut him short. She sat up in bed, and while he watched, she arranged her hair. Then she picked up the pillow on which her head had reclined. She got to her feet.

'Where are you going?'

No answer. Without a word she opened one of the sliding panels. It was clear that she was deserting him, that she was moving her bed to the room of Ichiro and Sakiko.

'Hey, you. Come back!' yelled Jinpei. He screamed. No answer. He realized that again, in his own house, he was rejected by everyone. 'Hey, you! . . . Hey, you!'

When Jinpei's glassy eyes rolled open, he was only dimly aware of the young doctor's face set close to his own. The doctor peered intently at Jinpei's pupils. Jinpei could feel the back of his head throbbing with pain. With all his might he tried to move his tongue in speech. His tongue was useless, the words never came. He wanted to get well, to make amends for his life. Unexplainably, a morose vision of the face of Dr Koriyama grazed his field of awareness. There was to be no time for reparation.

January was now half over, and gone completely were the straw festoons and the other New Year's decorations. Fair weather prevailed for days on end and the streets were dry. On the façade of the Mitsukoshi Department Store was hanging still another sign to announce the Special February Sale.

'He's dying.'

The young doctor said it. Taka, Ichiro, and Sakiko took a close look at the yellowy face of Jinpei, whose eyes were closed in coma. Among the unshaven bristles on his chin they saw new grey whiskers showing. During the night the hairs had grown suddenly longer.

At the sight of the dying face, Sakiko thought of the word 'Methuselah', a word from the title of some article she had read a long time ago. She looked at her husband and her mother-in-law, both of them tense and silent. The young doctor was blinking his eyes. He made a silent bow from the hips and left the room, signalling the nurse to follow him with the camphor injection kit.

It was a windless, cloudless day towards the end of January, on the afternoon that witnessed a final drawing of the curtain over Jinpei Suda's sixty years of life.

The men were dressed in awkward-fitting cut-aways, and the women were dressed in black kimonos matching the mood of their solemn faces. They passed in single file through the great gate of the Myozen Temple in Teppo-machi. Just inside the gate to the temple grounds stood a table attended by several young men from the Weather Service. The table held a registry book and a box to receive the condolence gifts.

As the mourners passed through the gate, they wrote their names in the registry and then moved along towards the main temple building.

Each guest pulled up at the end of a queue that formed inside the temple and when his turn came, he clapped his hands together once, facing the cloud of incense smoke that enshrouded the sanctuary. The shadowy Buddhist altar was adorned with a photograph draped in wide black ribbon. To either side of the altar, rigid and reverential, the chief mourners sat on their heels and kept their hands on their knees. They were Taka and Ichiro and Sakiko; and opposite to them were the chosen representatives of mourning friends, Observatory Chief Sugé and City Councilman Aiba. Each time one of the participants stepped forward to clap his hands, the principal mourners made their acknowledging bow in perfect unison.

The Jinpei in the photograph wore an absurdly serious face. The portrait was obviously nothing more than the enlargement of an old snapshot, the features being fuzzy on the edges. Nevertheless Jinpei's angular face and the meticulous set to his buttonlike eyes were enough to stimulate the guests to instant recall of the whole man.

When everyone had taken his turn at lighting a joss stick, the whole assembly felt the relief that follows discharge of a duty. They gathered together in little groups, each to his liking, in some nook of the garden or under some venerable camphor tree, chatting politely, puffing at cigarettes.

In every group the talk began with the fatal illness of the deceased, then moved to symptomatic details of the low blood pressure which led to his breakdown and then to a softening of the brain.

'Does that ailment differ any from *high* blood pressure?' With a half-scared look on his face one of the older men addressed his question to the others in his group.

'The two are very much alike, they say, and yet there is quite a difference.'

'I tend to be underweight myself, so I've always felt easy about high blood pressure. But a man can never afford to be off his guard.'

The sky began to cloud over. A man wearing one of the black arm-bands hurried off to use the telephone.

By and by a little fleet of shiny black cars pulled up to the lofty temple gate along with the hearse. The twenty or thirty guests who were scattered about the temple precincts began to line up in the flagstoned area to await the removal of the coffin. A sexton lugged a box of tools into the sanctuary.

Even the guests near the temple gate could hear the banging noises raised when the relatives and the few close friends hammered in the coffin nails with a raw stone. The young men from the Observatory served as pall bearers, heading the procession that slowly descended the steps leading out from the sanctuary. As the coffin passed between the guests a few of the older women dabbed at their cheeks with handkerchiefs already damp. Were they weeping for Jinpei? More likely it was just the gloomy mood to be acknowledged at any funeral service.

Noiselessly the cortège glided away, the hearse followed closely by the three black rental cars. The first car carried the principal mourners, Ichiro and Taka and Sakiko and the younger son in junior high school. The other two cars held relatives who had come from different parts of the countryside, along with the representative friends like Sugé and Aiba.

Having arrived at the crematorium beyond the city limits, the party gathered together in the superintendent's little house to wait for Jinpei's incineration.

The sky, which had begun to cloud, now cleared again. Still wearing their cut-away coats, the men stood warming their hands around the brazier in an eight-mat room. They began to discuss again, for the umpteenth time, the ineluctable topic of low blood pressure leading at last to softening of the brain. Taka gave instructions to Sakiko and to some women relatives on how to arrange on the bare round table the tier of nesting lunch boxes which they had brought. Then the women moved about, pouring tea in everyone's cup.

'I am so grateful for your being with us today.'

Each time that Taka paused to express her personal thanks to each individual guest, dutifully each individual guest related to her again his recollections of Jinpei and of Jinpei's grand achievements.

'Indeed I feel that we have lost an irreplaceable man.'

In the middle of the gathering stood Aiba, dressed as was his personal preference in Japanese kimono, and wearing his Inverness cape.

'A man of his calibre – with us no more. It's a shame. I've always thought I couldn't get along without his help and his

advice in all sorts of problems connected with the new hotel.'
He gripped the tea cup in his fat hands, and slurped at the brew
in sibilant approbation. 'More than anything else I wanted our
departed friend to publish a book of his studies on Akadaké.'

'Oh?'

Observatory Chief Sugé wheeled around in the councilman's
direction. The Chief noticed that his pin-stripe trousers were
getting baggy at the knee from crouching down near the *hibachi*.

'I'm surprised. Suda Kun – he had in mind to write a book on
Akadaké?'

'That's what I was saying.'

'I hadn't heard about it.'

'Probably not. There was a problem about paying for the
printing, so I suppose he never mentioned it.' In quiet exultation
Aiba looked from face to face at everyone in the room. 'But I
never hesitated for a moment, happy to pledge anywhere from
twenty to thirty thousand yen to publish his privately under-
taken research. I thought that a book like that would be very
helpful in advertising the tourist value of our city.'

The matter of including direct publicity for the new hotel, the
matter of having himself be commissioned to write the Foreword – he never mentioned the tough negotiations of that night,
he never mentioned that he had been shrewd enough to impose
these two conditions on Jinpei. He emphasized exclusively how
he himself had been ready to support a fellow townsman
scientist.

'At any rate – if we limit discussion to Akadaké – there has
been no one to match the work of Suda Kun.'

'You mean the Akadaké Demon?'

Chief Sugé wore a thin ironic smile on his concave cheeks.

'Suda Kun's research at best was nothing more than a rehash
of the theory of Professor Koriyama. But give him credit. The
old chap did a lot of climbing on the mountain. Don't they say
that even shortly before he died, he went out to the mountain
without a word to his wife?'

'Well, likely that's what killed him, wouldn't you say? At his
age, and sick as he was, he still wanted to grapple with the

mountain. Nevertheless, it's thanks to him that we were able to proceed with confidence in building the hotel.'

Here again Aiba failed to mention how he had pressured the sick man to guide him up as high as the Sixth Station on that particular day towards the end of the year. Instead, his voice went sentimental.

'Almost on the point of death, his going up on the mountain – maybe he went out there to bid a last farewell to Akadaké.'

All the other guests, hands resting on their knees, were listening in formal deference to this exchange between the councilman and the chief. There wasn't a soul among them who doubted that Suda had offered his life on behalf of Akadaké. And yet, by this hour, the whole assembly was fed to the gills with commemorating the departed one. Since the preceding night they had been forced to hear the story over and over again. Inevitably then the talk slid away on the tangent topic of the new hotel that Councilman Aiba would establish.

'The idea is this. We have to attract lots and lots of visitors from abroad, so I'm planning to furnish it in the latest American style.'

But this was the moment when Taka put her head in the room to announce that the cremation part of the funeral was complete. A few of the relatives rose to their feet to go and fetch the bones.

The bones already rested in a crock, but it had been decided to inter the burnt out ashes on Akadaké. Jinpei used to tell his colleagues at the Weather Bureau, just for a joke, that he wanted his ashes buried on the volcano. He had asked for it himself.

What he had intended as a joke was taken for a serious wish of the deceased. The very fact that Jinpei was the old man called the Akadaké Demon was enough to persuade the Weather Bureau staff that it was their duty to carry out the request.

Aiba too, when he appeared at the wake the night before, had offered his own suggestion. 'Whatever you do, please bury the remains on the site of the Akadaké Hotel. After all, it's the least I can do.'

It did no harm for the city councilman to have the ashes

interred on the hotel grounds. Quite the contrary, he was eager to prove to the family of Jinpei and to the Weather Bureau, how very highly he treasured the departed, how profoundly he mourned his passing.

The bus went panting up the steep incline strewn with volcanic ash and pumice. It was the bus that Jinpei had ridden in the past on his numerous visits to the island. Seated in the bus were the immediate family, along with Aiba and Chief Sugé, and a few of the younger men from the observatory who had helped in the funeral ceremonies, chaps like Kato and Kinoshita.

Akadaké showed in sharp detail against the clear blue sky, as it had done on that autumn day when the dead man observed his formal retirement from public service.

The red leaves had already fallen from the sumac trees, and from the clumps of barren trees one might catch now and then a cracking noise that sounded almost like a falling stone. The volcano appeared to be looming close over all of them by the magic of some optical illusion.

Ichiro carried the crock of ashes on his lap, flanked on either side by Sakiko and Taka. The crock was neatly wrapped in a white cloth. Every time his eyes happened to fall on it, Ichiro couldn't avoid thinking again of his departed father.

'The funeral stipend was way too high,' he whispered to the old woman. 'How about the retirement bonus, Mother . . . I suppose it's all gone?'

Taka's eyes remained closed. She said nothing. Ichiro thought that perhaps she was feeling car sick from the ride.

'I just thought of something – a good idea about the condolence gifts. Let's suppose that the people gave us their money only intending to cover our costs for the funeral.'

'You're crazy,' Taka said, eyes suddenly open. 'The mourners expect the usual return gifts. We have to do it, and it's going to cost us more than we can afford.'

Twilight was beginning to signal its approach. The sky was clear, but the winter sun, which turned the slopes of Akadaké to the colour of elephant hide, was gradually becoming less brilliant. The single plume of yellowish smoke was drifting slightly towards the north.

'The mountain is really peaceful,' offered Aiba, removing his Inverness cape. He had taken a seat on the opposite side of the bus. 'Whenever I see the mountain as it is today, I feel that I come to share the sentiment of Suda Kun.'

Unquestionably the mountain was peaceful today, even without the councilman's endorsement.

The pale light of evening's approach, the silent plume of volcanic smoke rolling against the sky, the tones of grey in the mountain's hide touched the sensibilities of all. But most of all it was the melodramatics of coming to lay in final repose on the mountain the mortal remains of the old man who had loved the mountain more than any other. It moved the hearts of all towards mawkishness. And yet young Kato, and Kinoshita too, were quite aware that come tomorrow they would clean forget the former Section Head. Eventually there would come a time when the name of Jinpei Suda would never again be mentioned at the Weather Bureau.

When the bus stopped on Point Shimoné at the Third Station level, the whole party gave precedence to Ichiro in filing off the bus. Then in no particular order they started walking up the mountain road that was roughly scattered with pumice.

'Ichiro Kun, your father was a wonderful man, don't you think?'

The councilman fell in step beside the son who was plodding along while he clutched the crock with both hands.

'This mountain will never erupt again. Your father proved that much with his own two feet, fifteen years of it. When somebody told me that he went up the mountain almost on the point of death, I was struck with deep admiration.'

Ichiro bowed his head to acknowledge the compliment, but then his head jerked up in a quick glance at his wife Sakiko who walked with him on the other side.

Dressed in a black mourning kimono, Sakiko somehow looked younger.

And yet she was weary from the attentions she had been

forced to pay to the guests last night and today. Her colour was a little pallid.

'Right to the end Suda Kun maintained his unshakeable faith in Akadaké. For that alone he was a grand person.'

The councilman failed to mention it, but he was quite conscious within himself of that day when he had come with Jinpei to check on any emission of gas, after Jinpei had read Dr Maejima's essay. For a second time Ichiro turned his eyes towards Sakiko at his side. The faint smile crossed her face but only for a moment, just long enough for him to notice it.

The ground levelling at the hotel site was finished, but a couple of coolies were still busy feeding piles of accumulated brush into a bonfire.

'Here's the right spot.'

Aiba came to a halt. He looked in exultation at the others gathered in a circle around him. They stood at a place on the site from where they could see the mountain slopes beyond them still catching the pale light of the evening.

'We should have brought a shovel.'

Kato spoke his chagrin to Kinoshita.

'Well, maybe . . . I can dig with a tree branch.'

Kato hacked away at the tangled roots with a stick and stone till he had a one-foot hole. Ichiro placed therein the crock which he had been hugging to his breast.

With the crock in position, each person in the group tossed a handful of soil on top of it.

'This can serve for a marker, can't it?'

A young staff member broke out in a sweat as he rolled up a volcanic boulder lying nearby.

'Sooner or later we must set up a regular memorial stone on the spot.'

Chief Sugé turned the inevitable sardonic smile on this underling.

'Shall we inscribe it THE DEMON OF AKADAKE?'

'Chief, can we have a word of eulogy from you, something very brief?'

Being so requested by Aiba, Chief Sugé forced a little laugh, but Kato and Kinoshita immediately started clapping. They nudged Sugé towards the centre of the group.

The chief removed his hat and lowered his eyes to the ground. The lean figure of a man, the graduate of Tokyo University, seemed to be searching about him to locate some beautiful words and phrases.

'Suda San was called the Akadaké Demon. Now we are gathered on this very mountain which he himself ascended on more than eighty occasions since he assumed his office. When it comes to speaking for Akadaké, in the whole length and breadth of Japan there is no man to be compared to our departed friend. So every one of us from the Weather Bureau has always firmly believed, and now more than ever our belief endures.'

Sakiko, listening to his words, somehow could not suppress the smirk that rose again to her face.

The sun went down. The shades of dusk filtered through the site by imperceptible degrees. Still everybody in the group held on patiently, waiting for the chief's long speech to end. Then Akadaké herself, like the wing of some gigantic bird, cast over the slope the unmistakable shadow of evening dark, while peacefully continuing to emit her single pillar of smoke.

TEN

The afternoon sun flooding through the windows laid cross-striped patterns on the worn out linoleum floor of the hospital corridor. Durand left his room to head for the toilet, but he stopped in front of the room next door. He bent to reach the doorknob.

There had been not a sound from the room since the day before yesterday. Until the end of the old year he used to hear noises from the man whom they say had served in the Weather Bureau. Through the wall Durand would hear the old boy coughing. At times he might catch quiet snatches of conversation between the man and his wife. But never again after the night when they wrapped the old man's body in a sheet, loaded it on a stretcher, then hauled it away.

Noiselessly Durand twisted the knob and stuck his head into the vacant room. The window, white with dust, was half open. On the iron bed frame with the peeling paint lay nothing but a bare straw mattress. The empty mattress sagged in the middle to show where it had long sustained the sick man's body weight.

Durand stared at the empty sag for a long time.

Although he was next-door neighbour to the now deceased old man, Durand had never spoken to him in the hospital. The one time he did speak to him was New Year's Day, when Durand took it into his head to go out to Akadaké. On the excursion boat to Shirahama the woebegone old fellow sat in the third class cabin, shoulders hunched up higher than the faded muffler round his neck. Durand remembered that out on the deck, no sooner had he mentioned Akadaké than in a trice the old man sprang to life. Half bumptiously, half obsequiously he'd begun to prattle. Durand of course took little note of what the old man said. He had no particular interest, no particular respect for anything this Japanese might tell him. Cunningly he listened only enough to play the old man for a fool by cutting in to contradict what he said. Ten minutes later he had dismissed all thought of the fellow-patient from the room next door to his.

Nevertheless, musing now on the hollow sag in the straw mattress, Durand vaguely wondered about his neighbour's death – the man in the faded muffler, droopy-headed on the hard bench in the cabin, the man who ordered his wife around in whispers, the man with the hacking cough to mark the sickly daytime hours of hospital life. In some way or other the realization refused to come home to Durand that the other one had gone before him into death. He made an effort to picture how the old man might have died. It was like grabbing the empty air to snatch at some illusive, ominous spectre.

He heard footsteps approaching from down the corridor. Durand always knew from the sound itself if the steps were those of a doctor, a nurse or a patient. There was no mistaking these weary heavy ones, the slow drag in these feet. They were those of patients on the ward, beaten under the double burden of chronic illness and hospital routine.

'You know, I upset the whole thing . . .'

'What did you say?'

The patients treading the corridor were apparently two women.

'The powder medicine I got from Dr Tadokoro . . .'

'It was an accident . . .'

By and by the sound of the weary slippers faded out somewhere beyond the stairwell.

Durand touched his hand to the sag in the mattress. He felt that something faintly moist remained there. The faint residue, Durand realized, was not the actual sweat from feverish sleep. He detected something redolent of the poignant suffering of any man once he falls deathly ill. Those long sleepless nights, listening to the doleful howling of the dogs locked up in the vivisection kennels; eyes wide open, waiting in solitude for day to come, for windows to blanch; heaving sighs in spite of himself, from the fears of surgery, from fears for his family, from fears for his own livelihood.

Of course Durand knew hardly anything of the old man who had occupied the room, what sort of life he had led. He could not determine for himself with what frame of mind the man had faced up to death, nor in what manner he might have loved his wife and children. Nevertheless, drawing his fingertips through the lonely hollow in the mattress, he vaguely conceived that he and the other did have something in common. The same fate had stalked them both, driving them to the wall – the fate of old age. Both the man and himself, weighed down by the ugliness of age, had been waiting day by day for Death, till at length the other man had said goodbye to Age.

Durand felt that the mattress hollow bore the death impression of the man who had lain there. The impression was not all that deep, not all that sad, not all that heart-rending. Had the man expired gently, without a struggle? In time another patient would be brought in. Some member of the family would help the nurse's aid to lay a pad of cotton stuffing on the mattress, then spread over it the hospital sheets worn thin from uncountable laundry trips. By that time doctors and nurses would have completely forgotten the previous occupant of the bed.

Could he only bring it off, Durand wished to die in the manner of the Japanese. He wanted death to be painless, a mere surrender of his frame to its own debility, like gliding into heavy sleep. But such an ending to his life was not to be, and he knew it.

Each time he came to think of dying, invariably a certain vision of horror besieged him. At this very moment he tried mightily to drive away his own childish image of hell. Ever since he had turned his back on the Church, this tormenting fear of hell lurked never far below his threshold of awareness. The fear had been planted in him as a child. He fought against the fear, but no matter what he tried he could not suppress it. The terror of being punished by God, the horror of suffering eternal torture, stayed with him during the day, but more so in the deep of night, when he could wake from sleep at any moment with a nightmare vision of the horror come upon him like a

storm. At such a time his howling was never loud, but howl he
did like a dog. The howling issued from pain that clutched his
chest like a vice. He would sit up in the dark, open-eyed and
motionless, waiting for the pain to slowly ooze away.

In the better years of his life there were times when Durand
admitted to himself that his idea of hell was quite absurd. He
tried to believe that anything like a world of the damned, identi-
fied as hell, was nothing more than some figment of the imagination invented by the Church to restrain the faithful by fear. At
any rate, in the later part of his life, try as he might, he could
never escape the fear that his deeds were going to be punished.
It could be that his fear of punishment was linked in some way
to the medieval panorama of hell depicted in a print that hung
in the library reading-room at the minor seminary where he
went to school.

Of course he wasn't quite so naïve as to accept the picture
as literal truth – to believe that hell was an enormous dungeon
underground, where unquenchable flames enfolded writhing
masses of naked men and women, where the devils flailed at
them with cat-o'-nine-tails. Nevertheless, he quaked still more
with fear precisely because he could not foreknow the way in
which the wrath of God was going to fall on him.

He feared death because he feared the pains of hell. Merely
to take one's leave of life was something to be wished. The
sooner the better, he thought, to be freed from people's white-
eyed stares, from Father Sato's hand-outs, from the old age
that he spent in picking open with his fingers all the old sores.
But he feared dying because he feared going to hell.

Durand knew that Jinpei Suda, being a Japanese, had no
reason to be tormented by any notions similar to his own. He
felt a touch of envy for Jinpei, along with a futile resentment.
He pressed his head against the dingy window pane.

'Sacré vieux chien . . . Sacré vieux chien . . . Sacré vieux
chien . . .'

The noontime streets lay sleepily quiet under the winter sunlight. Durand saw taxis and lumber trucks moving up and down
the boulevard lined with palm trees. Outside the windows of
the apartment houses he saw row upon row of laundry hanging

out to dry. How many months – no, how many single days –
still remained to him for gazing at the familiar street scenes in
Japan? He wondered how many.

Towards the end of February the first unit of St Theresa's Villa
was ready. The dining-room and kitchen were not yet built, but
for the moment the right wing, housing chapel and assembly
room, was ready.

At Mass on a Sunday in February Father Sato had announced
to the Christians a parish excursion to view the new chapel.
The plan was to offer Mass at the church in Kuratacho at 7.30
in the morning, after which Father would join with the Christians
who wanted to go, board the excursion boat for the island, and
carry out a ritual blessing for the new building at St Theresa's
Villa.

A great turn-out of parishioners, beyond his expectation,
went out with Father Sato for the ceremony of blessing. He
was enormously pleased. On the boat ride over the peaceful
sea the fellows from the Young Men's Club stood in a huddle
close to him. He wore his white Roman collar. The boys had a
supply of candles and other sacred items for the new retreat
house. The matrons of the Ladies' Sodality were chatting pleasantly one with another. They were bringing individually wrapped
boxes of rice balls, a treat reserved for after the rites of
blessing.

'Father, the *Catholic News* has quite a write-up about you.'

The *Catholic News* is a paper that reports for the faithful once
a week on Catholic affairs around the world, and gives news of
Church activities within Japan. It was the pride and joy of any
Catholic to have his own parish featured in the paper along with
a picture of the pastor.

'Well I'll be darned! I never knew a thing about it.' Father
Sato roguishly pretended ignorance.

The fact is, however, that with mouth and cheeks bathed in
smiles he had read the piece early this morning in the privacy
of his room. He had read it over and over to the point where
he almost memorized each ideograph and every turn of phrase.

'Haven't you seen it yet? Here, the article's on page three, and your picture too.'

One of the lads reached up to hand him a copy over the shoulders of the group. Father Sato put on his reading glasses, then opened the paper while the group swung around to enjoy a peek from behind.

'Is this me? This fellow's a lot more handsome than the real thing.' The priest spoke in mock astonishment, then raised his voice for all to hear him read the account of St Theresa's Villa, the article he already knew by heart.

At the harbour of Shirahama he chartered two whole buses. During the ride, the priest attempted to collect his thoughts for the talk he would have to give. The Christians were all in fine fettle, as though they were going on a picnic. The kids raced up and down the aisle between the seats. He could call every one of them by name.

'Tsutomu, will you get First Communion next year?'

He grabbed the hand of one of the boys running in his direction, then he swung around to look towards a seat further back in the bus.

The boy's mother, one of the Sodality ladies, answered with happy deference. 'I've been wanting to ask you if it couldn't be even this year, at Easter,' she said.

'I understand.'

The priest found personal satisfaction in his position as father to the big family that constituted his parish. While he relaxed in the vibrating bus, he felt more than ever the mellow consolation of being idolized and loved by all.

Akadaké was emitting its wisp of smoke against a cloudless firmament, the vapour rising to lose itself in the dazzling blue of the heavens. Suddenly there flitted through his mind the sneering face of Durand.

'He's a crazy one,' he thought, 'twisted heart and soul, can't face the facts . . .'

Durand had stubbornly clung to the belief that Akadaké was going to erupt. On an occasion like the present, however, Father Sato could well afford the pity he felt for Durand's recalcitrant heart. Were it possible, he would even lead the man to

St Theresa's Villa, where in nature's serene pure air he would try to straighten out the kinks in Durand's soul.

When the two chartered buses finally reached their destination, the Christians formed a procession and started up the hill. The cross atop a tiny steeple on the unpretentious building first came in view through the barren branches of an intervening copse. Immediately the children up in front let out a yell and began to run ahead.

'Don't run! Hey, no running!' The members of the Young Men's Club spread their arms to hold the children back. There was the danger of falling on the pumice stones and the volcanic rocks that littered the earth.

'What do you think? It seems to be just right . . . ,' said Father Sato with satisfaction while he used a handkerchief to wipe the sweat from inside the collar of his cassock. His satisfaction was complete, looking back to memories of the many obstacles overcome to make the cherished dream come true at last.

'You really did a tremendous job,' said one of the Christians, quick to interpret the priest's remark as fishing for compliments. 'I never dreamed you could raise a magnificent structure like this.'

'Thank the good Lord, who never fails to come to our help if the cause be worthy.'

'So . . . today that's the line I'll take in my talk for the Christians,' he thought. 'I must show them how the gate will always be opened, how God will never fail to answer the prayers of His faithful.'

Arriving finally at the chapel the Christians crowded close around the priest as he inserted a huge key in the door. The pungent odour of varnish wafted from the ten-*tatami* room. The wood veneer on the walls and ceiling was not yet thoroughly dry. Had a winter housefly been taking shelter in the room? A big one wheeled about, banging its head against the window panes that were still flecked with spatters of fresh white paint. Since neither an altar nor any other furnishings were yet in place, the priest stood directly in the middle of the room and began to sprinkle holy water for the ceremony of blessing.

The ritual completed, Father turned to face the Christians with a happy smile on his full-fleshed cheeks.

'Today is a day to remember, for it is the day on which all of you take possession of this house. It goes without saying that when I use the word "possession", the meaning is vastly different from the usage of people in the world. The "possessions" I refer to are spiritual possessions . . .'

He paused for a long and earnest look at the faces of the men and women gazing up at him.

'For years I have been thinking ahead to our possessing this home imbued with the pure happiness of heaven itself right here in the open natural environs of Akadaké. All of you are acquainted with the vast numbers of holy Christians who in the early ages of the Church went out to the wilderness, where they built monasteries to follow lives of prayer and contemplation. But unfortunately for ordinary people like us, we cannot follow their example perfectly. The lives we lead are stained with the evils of the world and we are encumbered with the heavy cares of earthly existence. For that very reason, we have need to live in a holy place such as this though it be for only a few days in the year. This was the reason for my establishing St Theresa's Villa.'

With folded hands resting on his barrel chest, the priest continued speaking. 'We can purge our hearts of sin. That is the end for which St Theresa's Villa will be of benefit to all.

'Akadaké is a mountain which in days of old exploded with violent eruptions. But in the present age it has changed to an utterly peaceful mountain. We can think of Akadaké as a symbol of the thing that we call sin.' Somewhere in a corner of his awareness came a vision of Durand's sweaty face and the thin smile on his cheeks. 'All of us, in the manner of this mountain, can wipe out our inclinations to evil, lay aside our sins. What is more, we must make the effort to do so.'

The little children up front were showing signs of restlessness, poking fingers into their noses, beginning to twist and turn. Mothers struggled with both hands in futile attempts at suppressing them. Now there were a number of houseflies on the wing, bumping and buzzing against the window panes.

That was the moment when the assembly caught the jerky noise of someone kicking off his shoes in the entrance way. Standing in the chapel door was old Mr Toshimitsu, who helped out part-time at the church as general factotum.

'Father, please.' His face was strangely earnest while he raised a hand to signal secrecy.

'What is it? Right now?'

'Please . . .'

Breaking off his talk, Father Sato followed old Toshimitsu out of the door, where the dazzling sunlight hit him full in the face and made his eyelids quiver, which only exaggerated the mystified look he gave the old man.

'When did it happen?' he whispered in a shaken voice.

'Last night, apparently. But it wasn't discovered until sometime this morning. That's what they said.'

'What a mess! I can't return right this minute, and I can't announce bad news like this to the Christians – not at a special time like today. But anyway, you too, keep quiet about what happened. Please.'

'I know what you mean.'

He returned to the chapel and continued his talk, trying hard to disguise the turbulence inside him. When it finished, the ladies of the Sodality and some of the girls began to distribute the individually wrapped packages full of rice balls. The plan was for the people to eat their lunches at any spot they wanted on the grounds of St Theresa's Villa.

'Father, here's a big one for you,' said one of the ladies, laying in his hands a really massive, specially wrapped package. 'You're pretty heavy, so you have to eat a lot.'

When everybody laughed, even Father Sato went along with the spirit of it, trying to fix a smile on his cheeks. The effect, however, was more like an ugly contortion.

'Listen, everybody, I'm awfully sorry, but Toshimitsu San has just brought word that a very important guest has appeared at the rectory.' His voice was serious. 'I have to hurry back alone. I'll have the president of the Young Men's Club take over the arrangements. So please, all of you, enjoy yourselves. Have a really good time.'

Then with a weird expression on his face, Father Sato made
his way through the people sitting on the floor. Every pair of
eyes followed him out of the door. He met with Toshimitsu and
headed for the road.

Not before they were settled in the taxi Toshimitsu had
engaged for the trip up was he able at last to heave a sigh of
relief.

'We have to contact the police . . . and the newspaper. The
paper could run a sensational story. If that should happen to
us . . .'

'Haa-a-ah . . .' Toshimitsu bowed so deeply in agreement
that he had to brace himself by putting both hands on the back
of the driver's seat in order to get himself upright again.

'The man has quite a history, you know . . . if we let the
sensational part come out in print, it will scandalize the Christians, and . . .'

Not much more than an hour before, he had driven up the
Akadaké mountain road in high spirits. Now he was forced to
descend the mountain road in a mood of heavy depression. As
soon as he got back to town, he would immediately rush to
the hospital, from where he would try to contact the Bishop's
chancery. He had to do everything possible to keep the story
from leaking out. Far more than any deep feeling, any pity
for Durand's suicide, what had really upset him was just the
botheration of it all.

On the return boat ride he stared at the water in silence with
Toshimitsu. The rays of the afternoon sun sparkled off the
gentle ripples of the sea that was as calm as an inland lake. Two
or three fishing craft slowly drifted past the excursion boat.
Suddenly he began to think about the evening on which he had
returned to the city on this same boat in the company of Durand.

'Anyway, if I can only control the situation now, I'll be rid of
the burden I carried so long, and . . .'

The change in circumstances all at once came home to him.
With Durand out of the picture, all the clergy in the diocese
would be rid of that troublemaker, who stuck in the craw of
every one of them. The story had passed from mouth to mouth
among the Christians, how Durand came to the church on

Christmas Eve deliberately to cause an ugly scene. Besides that, Father Sato himself would no longer have to disguise his contempt for this foreigner, nor suppress his mild detestation when he made those sick visits and handed him the presents he had brought. Come to think of it, had he not himself been long and secretly hoping for Durand to die?

'Crazy thought . . .' He was ashamed of entertaining it, yet equally he had to deny the thought in order to save his conscience. 'Anyway, I carried out every pastoral duty I had towards a former fellow-priest . . .'

When they reached the boat landing, they hailed another taxi and hastened to the hospital. Whatever happened, he had to prevent its leaking to the papers and thus becoming another source of scandal.

He thought he recognized a company car from the newspaper parked in front of the hospital, but once he got inside, to his relief, everything appeared quite normal with the usual entrance-way congestion of ambulatory patients and many visitors. The movement of staff employees and nurses up and down the corridor was the same as ever.

'Don't you think we ought to speak to somebody in charge first?' asked old Toshimitsu.

'I was thinking so too.'

With an apprehensive look on his face Father Sato started walking down the main floor corridor.

He found the hospital superintendent busy with another guest and had to wait outside the office. Through a corridor window he looked out on a treeless inner courtyard where a couple of men in sterilized whites were throwing a baseball back and forth.

Pensively he fell to recalling the old days at the church where Durand was the pastor and he himself was the hard-working curate. Durand was little more than forty at the time. He cultivated a brown goatee, and with his deep-sunk eyes he kept to himself, holed up in his room. At dinner they sat together at table but rarely exchanged a word while Durand plied his spoon with his eyes glued to the magazine or paper lying next to his plate.

After that period Father Sato never really knew what Durand was thinking. He never had an inkling of the frame of mind that led to last night's action. But after what had happened, one thing was clear – this foreigner, who had failed as a man and as a priest, was finally about to slip from everyone's memory. There are sins in this world which simply have to be covered up, he thought. Durand was decidedly one of those sins.

Holding an overcoat over his arm the other visitor emerged from the hospital superintendent's office. The priest arranged a smile on his face before knocking at the door.

The superintendent was a short, balding, pleasant sort of man, but he was startled for a moment, scrutinizing the figure of Father Sato dressed in his cassock.

The conference turned out to be easier than expected. The superintendent said that somebody outside the hospital had already been in touch with him, that the hospital had also decided earlier to dispose of the matter without attracting public attention.

'But anyway, because the man in question was a foreign citizen, we also had a telephone call from the Consulate . . .'

And because it was a strict regulation to submit to a coroner's inquest, the remains had been carted off to the police infirmary; but as soon as that was done, the police authorities too had consented to the fiction of death by natural causes.

'Even his doctor, I should tell you, was reporting that the patient would live for only another two or three years, but the doctor never suspected that he would die by hanging himself. I suppose he brooded too much about his illness.'

According to the superintendent's account, Durand's door was ajar this morning when a passing nurse happened to glance inside and saw this huge body sprawled on the floor. He had fastened a cord to the bedpost and then around his neck, and like that he fell face up from the bed in such a way as to strangle himself.

'His body was enormous. I ran up there right away, and his body was enormous. I think foreigners in general tend to be heavier than one might think at first sight.'

Father Sato heard out the explanation with courteous attention.

The superintendent said he had put together the articles left in the room and given them to the police. As for Durand's personal effects, they were nothing more than a few suits of underwear and other pieces of clothing. It wouldn't take more than a single suitcase to haul away the lot.

'Could I be allowed to see the room?' asked Father Sato.

As they emerged from the superintendent's office, there stood old Mr Toshimitsu waiting dejectedly in the corridor, obviously ill at ease.

'There's nothing to worry about,' said Father Sato. 'I told them how to handle it.'

Then leaving the good old man to remain where he was, the priest went upstairs – the stairs he had climbed a number of times to visit Durand.

'I suppose you feel relieved, Sato San.'

He heard somebody whispering close to his ear. It sounded like the voice of Durand.

He shook his head, trying not to hear it. The time was getting close to evening. Beyond the fading light from the corridor windows he could see the distant blue of the water. Akadaké was purple. No doubt the Christians he had left behind at St Theresa's Villa were just about now getting ready to start for home. Durand had predicted that the mountain was going to explode. 'Because evil itself never dies out, does it, Sato San?'

But St Theresa's Villa was rising, and all had been carried off without mishap. The priest was leaning against a window from which he could gaze at the single plume of smoke rising from Akadaké.

GLOSSARY

Akadaké: 'Red Peak'.

futon: thick wadded quilts used for bedding when spread on a *tatami* floor.

gagaku: Japanese Imperial Court music in the ancient tradition.

geta: elevated wooden clogs.

go: the national board game.

hibachi: brazier for burning charcoal, used for warming hands and heating tea water. The traditional Japanese building has no central heating.

kotatsu: a square hole cut in the floor of a room; a low table is placed over the hole and a *futon* is spread over the table. Heat is provided by burning coals in the pit to warm the legs, hips and hands of people who sit on the floor and drop their feet down towards the level of the hot coals.

Kun: title used only in addressing males; less formal than *San*.

mochi: boiled rice of a high quality and very glutinous, which is thoroughly pounded, then shaped into cakes. A New Year's delicacy.

pechika: a type of coal-burning stove used in Manchuria.

San: title of respect, equivalent to Mr, Mrs, Miss, Ms.

Satsuma: traditional name for the old feudal province in southern Kyushu, now Kagoshima Prefecture. The fictional Akadaké and 'the city' of the novel are modelled on Mt Sakurajima and the neighbouring city and bay of Kagoshima.

Shogatsu: the three-day New Year holiday, January 1–3. The biggest holiday of the year.

tatami: floor mats about three inches thick. Packed with straw, the top side is finished with a smooth surface of woven reeds. Shoes are always removed before stepping on a *tatami* floor.

tokonoma: a narrow alcove raised several inches from the floor level of the room; used to display a hanging scroll, a flower arrangement or some other *objet d'art*.

toso: *sake* prepared with certain medicinal spices, supposed to purge the system of evil spirits and to promote long life. A New Year's speciality.

tsubo: a unit of measurement, roughly six square feet, the area covered by two *tatami* side by side.

zoni: a soup made with meat and vegetables in which is boiled a cake of *mochi*. A New Year's speciality.

SHUSAKU ENDO

FOREIGN STUDIES

Shusaku Endo, one of Japan's most distinguished and inter-
nationally renowned writers, eloquently charts the gulf between East and West in three linked narratives. Evoking Paris
in the 1960s, 17th-century Rome and provincial France in the
post-war years, he acutely conveys the frustrated alienation
felt by three Japanese students when confronted by the
spiritual values and culture of Europe.

'Endo has the major novelist's genius for making out of his
own and his culture's predicament works of art of wholly
universal relevance'
Paul Binding in The Listener

'A writer of remarkable power'
Francis King in the Daily Telegraph

'An immaculate, limpid moral tale, beautifully translated
into English'
Mary Hope in the Financial Times

'The whole novel gives a hauntingly authentic feeling of what
it is like to be foreign, to be a person apart. Each detail is
clearly observed and piercingly true'
Anthony Thwaite in the London Evening Standard

'Quite brilliant'
Ian Rankin in Scotland on Sunday

sceptre

ABEL POSSE

THE DOGS OF PARADISE

Winner of the prestigious Romulo Gallegos Prize for the best novel in Spanish over five years, this dazzling tale of the conquest of Latin America recreates Columbus' epic journey from boyhood in Genoa through decadent 15th-century Spain to the shores of the New World. Wittily weaving into the narrative analogies from later eras, Abel Posse offers a striking insight into a man who changed the world and a rumbustious, harsh yet haunting vision of his doomed search for an earthly paradise.

'An opulent, quick-witted masterpiece . . . a mobile novel which never clogs in its own riches. Posse springs light-footed over history's rubble. There's delight in his words and magic in his steps'
The Observer

'Only writing of the most royal purple, a translation worthy of it, and an irrepressible imagination could hope to do justice to such an historical phenomenon, and all three are sumptuously provided in THE DOGS OF PARADISE'
The Guardian

'Again demonstrates the superiority of Latin American fabulists over home-grown followers . . . Posse's passionate concoction appeals to all the senses and tells a moral tale, too'
The Independent on Sunday

'Powerful stuff . . . you will not forget the compressed fury and contempt that burst from every page, or the overwhelming sense of a Paradise Lost'
The Times

Selected and introduced by David Marcus

IRISH SHORT STORIES

Irish writers this century have excelled at the short story. Here David Marcus presents thirty-two outstanding and characteristic examples of their art, capturing the wit, scope and sheer entertainment provided by authors who range from George Moore and James Joyce to Neil Jordan and John McGahern.

'Shows a consistency of talent that seems almost unfairly bestowed upon one rather small land'
Janice Elliott in the Sunday Telegraph

'A very rich and varied collection, a real feast of a book'
Robert Nye in The Guardian

'The Irish are great lads at the short story, and here's another generously varied collection to prove it'
John Cronin in The Times Literary Supplement

'Excellent'
Gerry Colgan in the Irish Independent

'An excellent and definitive anthology'
Hibernia

'An impressive collection'
The Listener

'No one has done more than David Marcus to foster young and unknown talent, especially in this particular form . . . So the volume comes with the best possible credentials: and lives up to them in every way . . . a very important collection of magnificent work'
John Broderick in The Irish Times

sceptre